Praise for "THE ESCAPIST"

"Author David Puretz has created a highly literary and poignant work that tells many tales through its single-character narrative... *The Escapist* is an accomplished work worthy of great praise, both for its excellent writing style and its apt perspective on our current sociopolitical time."

–*Reader's Favorite 5-star review*

"The Escapist is a fast-paced novel about the miserable American road trip, sleeping outside of diners, failing to connect with hostile strangers and family members alike, and missing natural beauty for the chemical sunrise at the bottom of a pill bottle. Raising complicated questions about the nature of control, and drawing bold lines between state violence, family trauma, and self abuse, David Puretz has crafted a gut punch of a road novel for anyone who ever wondered what drove Hunter S. Thompson to drugs, and made Jack Kerouac want to leave it all behind for a dotted highway line."

–Chris L. Terry, author of the novels *Black Card* and *Zero Fade*

"Sizzling, a brilliant work of imagination…unflinching in its depiction of our culture and political moment…with the relevance and pace of Kerouac's *On the Road* and the psychological brutality of Golding's *Lord of the Flies.*"

–*Michelle Yasmine Valladares, MFA Program Director at The City College of New York, author of Nortada, The North Wind, and the AMERICAS Poetry Festival's Poet of the Year*

"A perfect time in our country for the return of the anti-hero. So many young men begin an odyssey into adulthood only to find that the past, usually in the form of a father, is both the catalyst forward and the keeper of a locked gate to the future. The goal becomes not salvation but survival. David Puretz's debut novel alternates between life's realistic blows and a hallucinatory journey that may be his only route to selfhood."

–*Linsey Abrams, author of Our History in New York, Double Vision, and Charting by the Stars*

"Crisp, clear, and electrically charged, *The Escapist* is a burst of much needed vitality blowing through the miasma of late capitalism's nihilism and hypocrisy."

–*Brendan Kiely, New York Times bestselling author of Tradition*

THE ESCAPIST

THE ESCAPIST

a novel
David Puretz

Global City *press*

THE ESCAPIST is a work of fiction. All incidents, dialogue, and characters, with the exception of some well-known historical and public figures, are products of the author's imagination and are not to be construed as real. Where real-life historical events or public figures appear, the situations, incidents, and dialogues are entirely fictional and are not intended to depict actual events or to change the entirely fictional nature of the work. In all other respects, any resemblance to persons living or dead is entirely coincidental.

Chapter 2 first appeared as a novel excerpt in *Legacies*, number 23, of *Global City Review*. An earlier version of Chapter 22 first appeared in the short story "Patriotism; An Homage to Yukio Mishima" published in *Promethean*.

Global City *press*

www.globalcitypress.com
Global City Press and colophon are
trademarks of Global City Press.

Copyright © 2020 by David Puretz
All rights reserved.

LIBRARY OF CONGRESS CATALOGING-IN-PUBLICATION DATA
Names: Puretz, David, author.
Title: The escapist : a novel / David Puretz.
Description: [2020 Global City Press edition]. | [New York, New York] :
    Global City Press, [2020]
Identifiers: ISBN 9781733359924 (hardcover) | ISBN 9781733359917
    (paperback) | ISBN 9781733359931 (ebook)
Subjects: LCSH: Young men--Mental health--Fiction. | Fathers and sons--
    United States--Fiction. | Drug addicts--United States--Fiction. |
    Escapes--Psychological aspects--Fiction. | LCGFT: Psychological
    fiction. | Thrillers (Fiction) | BISAC: FICTION / General. | FICTION /
    Literary. | FICTION / Psychological.
Classification: LCC PS3616.U76 E83 2020 (print) | LCC PS3616.U76 (ebook) |
    DDC 813/.6--dc23

Printed in the United States of America
Book design by Amy Veach. Cover art by Michael Puretz and Jaya Miceli.

The scanning, uploading and distribution of this book via the Internet or via any other means without the written permission of the author and publisher is illegal and punishable by law. Please purchase only authorized print or electronic editions, and do not participate or encourage electronic piracy of copyrighted materials. Your support of the author's rights is appreciated.

For Charlotte

PART ONE

1

Find Dad. Finally confront him about it. Confront him about everything. Use force if necessary. Find out how he got that eye gouged out. All those scars on his head. Was it from face-to-face combat? From shrapnel flying through the air from a roadside IED? From a bullet grazing his face? Make him reveal what he feels when he looks in the mirror. How unbearable it is to look. How unbearable it is that he's still here and so many of them are gone. That you're still here and that you still remember. That you'll never forget. Is that what made him run off? Did the volcanic pressure from all that buried shame finally cause this beast to erupt?

You'll find him and you'll hit him with the hard stuff. You won't wimp out this time. You'll go in deep. You'll go in for the kill. This time will be different. You had the chance the last time you saw him. You were sitting there with him at the table in Dundalk. It was silent. It was right there for you. But what did you do? You talked about badminton. Of course you did. How

THE ESCAPIST

you had started playing again.

--You're still playing that stupid fucking game, Shrimp?

That's how he said it. Fast and matter-of-factly.

--It's not stupid. It's fun. It's fun hitting people with the shuttlecock. I spiked it right into this lanky kid's face, and he stumbled and fell to the floor.

Dad's face didn't change. He didn't even acknowledge your response.

But then his blank face changed. You remember what made it change. It wasn't you. He would never change his face for you unless he was doing naughty. His face changed when he glanced out the living room window and saw one of the neighborhood kids on the front lawn holding a leash around a small dog's neck. The dog was dropping a large deuce right there on the lawn. Dad watched, shaking his head. The dog finished her business, and then the kid started walking away.

--What the fucking piss, Dad said.

Then he jumped out of his chair, ran to the front door, and then outside.

He yelled something at the kid. Something like: Hey, clean this shit off my yard! This is private property, you prick!

The kid chose to ignore him. The kid just continued walking away with his head down speaking softly to his pup.

Dad kept yelling at the kid: Stop, now! You will clean this shit off my property!

Still no response from the kid.

Then Dad bent down and picked up the piece of shit, picked it up with his bare hand, and chucked it at him. It hit him on the back of the head. Bulls-eye. The kid reached back, then looked at his fingers, realized what had just happened.

--What the fuck is your problem! the kid yelled as he turned back around.

He took a few steps toward Dad, but when the kid saw his face, saw that Dad was this one-eyed miscreant, he froze in place, bewitched by his presence. Dad did that to people. And Dad was staring at him, his eye locked on his target.

--My problem? My problem is little disrespectful fobbits like you leaving dog shit in my yard!

He yelled it with his back arched straight, his arms stiffly at his sides, his head bobbing forcefully forward.

--This little blue-head's out of formation, he said as he approached the kid.

--This little blue-head needs to learn some respect.

He had fallen back into it.

--What the fuck are you talking about, mister?

Then Dad grabbed him by his shirt.

--You shit in my yard? You shit in MY yard?

The pup picked up on his owner's fear and yapped and howled and danced around Dad's legs. The pup tried gnawing on Dad's pant-leg. Like a mosquito sucking the blood of an elephant. A nuisance, but not enough to sidetrack the beast from finishing his mission.

--I'm calling the police, the kid said in a cracking voice.

--I am the police, motherfucker.

He always said shit like that when he was back in it. The war. You came down the steps, ran over, and grabbed Dad by the shoulders. Dad jabbed back with his elbow and struck you square on the nose. You fell to the ground. Twenty years old, crying there on the sidewalk like a baby. God, you were a fucking pussy.

--Can we please just go inside? you pleaded, your pants a little piss-stained.

Dad turned his attention from the kid to you and helped you up. He brought you back into the house, sat you down on the couch, filled a bag with ice and rested it on your nose. The stench of dog shit permeated your breathing for hours.

Billy Chute put down the journal, amazed. He had intended to leave it blank. Yet he had begun writing. He was on the side of the highway, somewhere in western New York. Where? He couldn't see any signs. But this was his life again. Sitting in a car in the breakdown lane on the side of the highway. It's what Billy did best. Escape. Felix's farm where he had been working for the past couple of weeks had become a wasteland for him. Again. Like all of America was pure desert.

Billy had pulled his car over and written as Felix had requested of him. Keeping a journal, writing it all down, opening the pathways—it was Felix's last-ditch bid the morning Billy fled the farm to help this troubled boy he knew was maybe past saving. He saw something in Billy just as his daughter had, for it was Nicole that got him the job at the farm. It would have surprised Felix to know that Billy listened, took his advice to heart, that the words had just poured out of Billy into this journal which Felix had slid into his hands earlier that morning as he was fleeing, and the anecdote about his father was Billy's beginning.

"Game over," he finally said aloud, shaking himself out of a trance; he couldn't just park forever on the side of the highway. "Go to Grandma. Start there. And while you're at it, go see Uncle George. Uncle George'll let you stay the night. And Peter. Go see Peter too. That fucker. And Cynthia. No. Not Cynthia." The thought of seeing his step-mother made him suddenly want to shrivel up. *She won't be able to help you. She could never help you. She couldn't even help herself.*

He turned on the ignition then opened up the cooler on the floor of the passenger seat. It contained several pill bottles and nondescript bags partially concealed by plastic bottles of water and Gatorade and a towel. He removed the towel to wipe the sweat off his face, took out one of the water bottles and a pill bottle, removed two yellowish capsules, washed them down, and was on the move again. Billy drove south through rural New York, through Pennsylvania, into Maryland, chain smoking and switching radio stations between heavy metal, pure hits of the 80s, 90s, and today, and droll British public broadcasting voices. He got off the highway at the edge of Baltimore County and drove along the eastern banks of the Chesapeake Bay. When he got to Merritt Boulevard, to his old neighborhood in Dundalk, he saw the same buildings boarded up, the same fast food joints and gas stations exactly as they had always been, like the place was frozen in time. He slowed his car down as he passed the two-family duplex where he had grown up. It had been almost a year since he'd been back. The lawn was overgrown, and the tree in front was still rotting from the inside out, its limbs and branches sparser. The sidewalk was still uneven cement.

A horn sounded behind him.

From the car, he couldn't see Cynthia through the window, couldn't tell if she was inside. But with her bad back and lack of mobility, and most likely an even more bitter depression, it would have been rare for his stepmother to be elsewhere. She did have a job, but it was at night. He might have pulled his car over, parked, gotten out and even gone inside to see her, to confront her, too. But there was a driver behind him, a driver with a loud horn, and that horn was a bolt to his consciousness, a shock to his system, a sign to keep driving.

He continued west through downtown Baltimore. Billy drove up to his Uncle George's house in Towson, a quaint house on a quaint street in a quaint suburb of the city, parked the car, sat and stared into the windows of the house a while. He got out, stretched his legs and his back, and then rested against the hood. A car eventually pulled into the driveway. Aunt Tracy.

"Billy? What are you doing here?"

"Hey Aunt Tracy."

She walked over to him and gave him a hug. Then she pulled back to inspect him. "I haven't seen you in so long! God, look at you! You're all grown up! You look more like your father every time I see you."

"Can I stay the night with you guys?" Billy asked. "I came to visit Grandma."

After pausing for a moment, for he had caught her off guard, she said that she thought it would be okay. "You're just going to stay the night, huh."

"Yes, just for the night. I hope I'm not intruding."

"No, not intruding at all. Not at all! Come on inside, Billy-boy."

At the stairs to the house, Aunt Tracy looked back at him while fumbling for her keys. "Greg'll be home. He's back from college. He loves college. He's studying marketing, you know. He'll be so happy to see you."

"Marketing, cool."

They walked in, and Billy took a seat on the couch. Aunt Tracy went upstairs to put her stuff down. Billy could hear her talking in a low voice but couldn't make out the words. She eventually came down with Greg following behind her.

"Greg, look who it is! Cousin Billy!"

"Hi Greg."

"Hi Billy."

"Where's Uncle George?"

"I just spoke to him on the phone. He's still at work,

but I told him you're here. I told him you're staying the night. He suggested we all go out for dinner. A real nice dinner. How does that sound, Billy-boy?"

× × ×

Uncle George had found God later in life. He thanked God before each meal. Aunt Tracy closed her eyes alongside her husband and appeared to be in some kind of reverie, hanging off each word of his prayer. It struck Billy how different things would have been if his dad had also found God; then he wondered how one goes about finding God in the first place, where to look. *Do you find God or does God find you? Or do you just bump into each other somewhere on the side of the road and strike up a conversation, become friends, fall in love?*

Billy stared forward at Greg who was staring at the wall; neither of them blinked. Greg said "amen" along with his parents. As they ate, Billy followed along. There were many moments of silence interrupted by humdrum conversation. Uncle George and Aunt Tracy talked about work. Greg sat quietly, played with his food and made intermittent bites. Billy also did a form of food playing, yet his was more like food arranging, separating each food item into its own neat pile on the plate without letting any of the piles touch. Billy talked about his job at Cobin-Haskett in New York City and didn't mention that he had quit almost a month ago. Of course, they were scared to talk to him about anything real, especially about his dad. They didn't want to talk about Cynthia either. No uncomfortable conversation. It was Uncle George's way. Just get the meal over with. Eat your food, go home, maybe put on a movie, go to sleep, send the boy on his way. Uncle George picked up the tab for dinner. In fact, Billy was counting on it. Getting a good free meal was worth the uncomfortable silences with family members who were more or less strangers with recognizable faces ascribed to a few old memories.

The next morning, Friday, Billy awoke and sat up in bed. He heard movement downstairs: feet shuffling on floorboards, hushed voices, doors opening and closing.

Uncle George called his name from downstairs. Billy opened the bedroom door and peaked out his head.

"Good morning. How did you sleep?"

"Fine."

"Good. Hey, listen, Aunt Tracy and I are off to work. Greg's still here, and we wrote out directions to the Frederick Nursing Home in case you need them. Have fun with Grandma."

"Thanks, Uncle George."

The front door shut loudly. Billy closed the bedroom door and got back into bed. He pulled the sheet over his body, up to his chin, and stared at the ceiling. Then he heard the downstairs door open again, heard the creaking of the stairs, and then a knock on the bedroom door.

"Come in."

The door propped open a few inches, and Uncle George stuck his head through the crack of it.

"Listen." Uncle George paused. "I just want to tell you…I want to tell you that I'm sorry about everything that happened with your dad."

George pushed the door open and slowly entered the room with his head down. "He must have gone through hell out there. I can't imagine what he had to have seen. What he had to have gone through."

He sat down at the edge of the bed by Billy's feet. "You know he and I, well, we've always had our differences. Your dad and I haven't talked in a long time, as you know. It's been, gosh, eight or nine years now. We've said some pretty nasty things to each other. Done some pretty nasty things to each other. Growing up, things were tough for us. Being a kid in Dundalk, with our dad, your grandfather…I sometimes forget how hard things were, not just for me, but for your dad, too. Especially for your dad. Alan hated your grandfather, and your grandfather hated him, too. Hated both of us. Probably because when he looked at us, he was seeing himself, was seeing something about himself. And only hate would make a man do the kinds of things he did to us."

Billy was all too familiar with the sentiments.

"I don't know how much Alan has talked about this, if he's ever talked about it, how much you know. Maybe you know none of it. But he took it out on us. Alan got the worst of it."

Billy wondered how much Uncle George knew of his own experience with his father. Maybe Uncle George had only assumed.

"It's funny," Uncle George said, "Alan still followed in your grandfather's footsteps. He also joined the army. Just as much as Alan needed to get away from him, in some weird way, I think he enlisted for him. To get closer to him. To understand. I ran away from the fire—your dad ran right into it. Head first. That's just the kind of man he is. Just like your grandfather. And your grandfather, he really had it tough after the war, too. He was also injured. Badly. And he was never the same. The war maimed him. He didn't die out there, but that's what did him in. We didn't understand that as kids. And it's still hard. But it's God's will."

Billy was still staring straight up at the ceiling.

"I just want you to know," Uncle George said, "I want your dad to know, that I hope he can get through." Then in a low voice, Uncle George continued: "I wanted to call him. I really did. I just never could do it. And now he's off, God knows where."

"I'm going to find him," Billy said. He had written down the same sentiment just a day ago in the journal Felix had given him, but it startled him to say it. The words were a surprise just as much to him as they were to Uncle George.

"Please let me know if you do," he responded. He put a hand on Billy's leg, gripped it and shook a few times, not making eye contact. "It was good to see you, Billy. Give Grandma a kiss for me."

Billy heard the stairs creak as Uncle George walked downstairs, back out the front door. Eventually Billy turned onto his side and his eyes affixed to an off-colored portion of the wall. He sighed, then reached down into his bag at the base of the bed and took out the journal.

✕ ✕ ✕

Those first few days, Dad would hardly get out of bed. A beard had started to grow on his face. He whimpered in his sleep. And laughed crazy-like in his sleep. You would peek into his dark bedroom and hear him talking about stuff in his sleep, about all sorts of shit. Boxes, underfed children, chicken coops, saleable materials, champagne, a bulletin board, carbon monoxide poisoning, nipples, firearms, circus animals. Other indecipherable things too.

One night he got up and walked around, still under the spell of sleep, and peed into the trashcan in the kitchen. He went out the backdoor and stumbled down the stairs and crawled under the porch and remained there until morning. He walked into the kitchen covered in dirt and then went back upstairs and got in bed. Cynthia had to wash the sheets again.

Back to the bottle when actually conscious. He nursed a bottle of

Jameson during daylight, and the bags under his eyes—blackened aqueducts. His eyeball would continually slip into the back of his head. Cynthia would call over to you, and you would come over to sit with them so she wouldn't have to be alone with him.

--Dad, can I get you some water or something?

--No, but I'll tell you what—you can get the fuck out of my house. How about that? I want to be alone with my wife. Fucking go back to New York already.

The coldness had always been there.

--I'm just going to hang out a bit more; keep you guys company, you said.

--Didn't you hear me you little shrimpfuck, I said get the fuck out of here!

You looked at Cynthia for guidance, and she nodded her head, which meant that yes, it would be better if you left.

You don't share this information. That's still the rule. What about Nicole? No, she doesn't need to know about any of this. She probably doesn't want to talk to you anyway after you left Felix the way you did. Why would she want to know about any of your family shit? Look at Cynthia. She tried so hard to understand what it was that her husband was experiencing, constantly nagging him to talk about it, but she would always give up. When he attacked her, she gave up for good.

2

Billy put the journal back into his bag, packed up his things, then downstairs waved goodbye to his cousin, said "peace out, Greggy-boy," and hopped into his '98 Nissan Altima.

He drove a little over an hour west to Frederick, in central Maryland, to the nursing home. It was right next door to the National Museum of Civil War Medicine, Frederick's most popular attraction, and Billy appreciated how both of these places were in the business of preserving old things.

Uncle George had told Billy the night before not to alert Grandma that he was coming to visit as it would only confuse her and that she would end up forgetting the date of his visit and call Uncle George to ask if Billy was okay and why he was not there yet. Instead it was best to simply show up, say between twelve and two, right after lunch, when she would most likely be at her best.

THE ESCAPIST

Billy entered the Frederick Nursing Center and told the woman at the front desk that he was here to visit Gracie Chute. The receptionist told Billy to leave his driver's license at the desk, perhaps in a measure to prevent Billy from escaping with the old lady and wheeling her to freedom. She made him put a sticker on his shirt that said "Guest" with his name below it. Easier for his grandmother to know him.

The receptionist gave Billy her room number. On the fifth floor, he walked down the hall, which smelled of urine, of course, and found his grandmother's room. To the left of the door, her name was emblazoned on a gold metallic rectangle. When Billy was working in the mailroom at Cobin-Haskett, he had had a similar nameplate inscribed with his name, outside of his workspace. He quit that job to escape that and other meaningless things. His poor grandmother, unable to walk or think for herself, was locked into her own hackneyed bureaucracy, not that different from the one Billy had recently escaped, and was now trapped within it until the day she died.

Her bed was neatly made, and pictures of relatives were on the walls, on a bulletin board above her bed, and in frames on top of the dresser. She had a faded black and white framed photograph of her two sons, Alan and George, when they were in their early twenties, looking not that much older than Billy was now. *Looking sharp, Dad, looking sharp.* There was a picture of

Billy and his brother, Peter, as kids with matching puffy white jackets, smiling though staring off in different directions. No Grandma though. Billy exited the room and walked back down the hall to a main corridor where orderlies were standing about next to a larger room with a TV blasting out at the dozen old people situated around it.

At a table in the corner of the room, a couple elders were playing what looked to be backgammon. Billy asked one of the orderlies where Gracie Chute was. She pointed to a woman bent over in a wheelchair facing the television. *The View* was blasting out of the TV. This was the show of choice for the orderlies, not the residents, Billy knew. Most of the residents were invalids, he thought of them, lost in their own minds, drooling out the sides of their mouths, sagging out of their wheelchairs. Or their heads were flapped back as if looking to the sky. Eyes closed or eyes open but gone. He wondered what was running through their minds. *Is it a dead silence or are there still small reverberating echoes that dance through these still bodies?*

Billy walked over to his grandmother and crouched on his knees in front of her, blocking her vision of the TV. Her eyes, though, had been facing elsewhere, slightly up and to the left. It seemed she didn't care for *The View* either.

"Hi Grandma."

She was 79 years old, younger than most of the

others. But she was just as wrinkled and lost, he thought. How long had it been since Billy had last seen her? Years upon years, no doubt. He just couldn't remember exactly when. She was there at home while he was growing up, and then she wasn't. Billy kissed her sagging, mildly hairy face. He sat down on a bench next to her.

"Hi!" She was so excited to see him, or, at least, to have a visitor. He could have been anyone and the response would have likely been the same. *This unadulterated happiness—why couldn't that have trickled down the goddam family line.* Her eyes lowered from Billy's and checked the name tag: Billy Chute. It clicked—grandson—and she got it.

"I was in the area and wanted to stop by and see you. Talk to you about some stuff. And make sure everything was all right. See if you needed anything."

"I'm alright. Same old. I'm feeling much better than I was. If you remember I wasn't doing so good earlier." Her voice was high-pitched, and she had developed a lisp because of her dentures.

"I actually never heard anything about it until yesterday. Uncle George told me about it. He said you had an accident coming off the elevator."

"Oh, George. I'll kill him. I didn't have an accident—Shirley pushed me into the door. The elevator door."

"Shirley? Who's Shirley? She pushed you into the elevator door?"

"She pushed me right into the elevator door."

"Well I'm glad you're feeling better."

"So wonderful that you came to visit me. Tracy was talking to me about you. I think it's so wonderful that you came to see me. You kids have so much love in your hearts."

We do?

As she said this, she cupped her hand around Billy's cheek and stared deeply into his eyes. The moment came and went and Billy felt nothing—no sense of nostalgia, no lump in the throat. But he recognized it was a genuine moment of affection.

"Grandma, can I talk to you about my dad?"

"George? I'll kill him."

"No, Grandma, George is your other son, my uncle. I'm talking about my father, Alan, your older son. Alan?"

"Alan, what a good boy. He works so hard for his family."

He does?

"Such a handsome man he turned out to be. We have such a beautiful family."

Beautiful?

"Yes, I guess we are an attractive bunch. Thanks to you! We have you to thank for that!"

She gurgled a laugh, getting a kick out of this.

While she was basking in this grandson-beauty, an orderly walked in to give patients their medications, their body and/or brain numbing formulas. *Could be nice when you're that old. Turn it off. Shut, the motherfucking thing off already.*

A flicker suddenly went off in his head. The tingling returned with forehead sweat and grinding of the teeth. The desire for drugs came flooding into his brain like three hundred wood chimes being struck by the same gust of wind that got progressively louder as they got closer to him, the sweet music turning into a steady swelling of sound. Even the TV seemed louder, and Billy dropped to his knees and grabbed onto the armrest of his grandmother's wheelchair.

× × ×

His grandmother had, in some respects, a similar practice of ritualistic drugging as he had, and in many respects, still sought. It was her routine Billy was seeing that brought him to his knees, even though months had elapsed since his own daily drugging rituals had slackened. They were at their most ceremonial during his reign at Cobin-Haskett back in New York.

His workday at Cobin-Haskett would come to an end, at the same time and in the same way as all his other days, with a final mail run through the building at 4:10, back to his desk at 4:45 and promptly out the back doors a few minutes later, unwilling to give them anything more than the eight hours of his day that he was contractually obligated to work. Billy would ride the N train across Manhattan to Astoria Boulevard. It was a short walk from the train stop to his one-room basement apartment. There would be only about half an hour of relaxation before he would start making his preparations. By half past six, latest, it would all be laid out in front of him on the coffee table, and then he would begin.

On weekdays he would smoke his pot, ingest multicolored opioid tablets, sip his whiskey, roll up his tobacco and smoke that too. His weekend ritual usually involved harder drugs, and toward the end of his last stretch in the city, his MDMA pharma-connect had disappeared, so he had to satisfy himself with the more accessible substances. He used cocaine, but, as one of his pharma-connects explained, if the South American climate was too cool and there wasn't enough moisture in the air, which had been happening more and more, the cocoa leaves couldn't flourish enough for proper benzoylmethyl ecgonine alkaloid extraction leaving them in short supply. He'd resort to breaking up some amphetamines he obtained through simple prescriptions. He was prescribed Adderall but also had easy access to Dexedrine and Ritalin, all of which were solutions Cynthia had found for her stepson's erratic behavior, and if he were to date it back, it could easily be said that Cynthia had Billy hooked before he reached double digits. Cynthia never considered how easy it would be for a young man to get his fingers on these Schedule IIs.

THE ESCAPIST

Billy had been over-prescribed his whole life. And Alan had been quick to hand-feed him meds of his own, especially late at night when Cynthia was at work. It was at his boarding school, Mission Mountain Prep, where he first tried heroin.

During this ritual, Billy would sometimes bump 20 milligrams up his nose. If he was in a rush to leave the apartment or had plans to go somewhere, he would have upped the dosage to 30 milligrams. There were unidentifiable pills in orange pill bottles with black permanent marker on their labels. The chemical makeup of these were unclear, as his sources informed him they could have been ecstasy, or meth, or an MDA/MDMA variant, or a combination of sorts. That didn't stop him from taking them. He welcomed the surprising impact and relief.

He would diagram out the properties of his narcotics and their effects onto sticky notes. They were placed on the right side of his coffee table in a rectangular formation, five by seven. A new collection had amassed which charted out new effects when substances were combined. His last couple of weekends during the stretch consisted of his mystery ecstasy, Adderall, and alcohol, followed by large doses of oxy later in the evening to help with the taper-off:

Amphetamine's absorption reduced with vitamin C/citric liquids. Less PH balance in stomach, stronger effect. Tums to counteract for maximum possible absorption. Ecstasy, perhaps placebo, but still I'm rolling. Part amph, part meth?

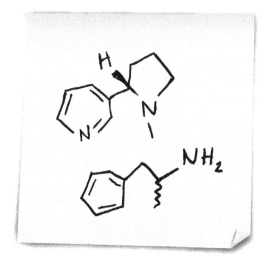

THE ESCAPIST

His last weekend bender while still under the employ of Cobin-Haskett turned into a longer, duller weekend than most with his narcotics withering within his bloodstream, and by Sunday morning, the high was still manipulating his sanity and his sense of right and wrong. Though oh so typically—the climax came and went, the best was gone, and he tumbled back into sobriety. His mind returned from its transformation. It returned from the state it was in before the drugs kicked in and turned him into something different, something of an existence he held of higher value than his unrigged self. On weekends like these, Billy liked to disassemble the pieces of the jigsaw puzzle that was his mind to explore potential identities, to maybe discover what he really wanted to be, what he could be, even if momentarily, to maybe discover how he wanted others to see him—to help him become something better.

When sleep eventually would come, his dreams would spoil because of the toxins, but it was during this sleep that his transformation back to normalcy took place. The toxins would be ciphered into his colon for disposal, the influence squeezed out of his head. He would wake and look in the mirror and for a split second he would see what he was and reminisce about what he had turned himself into. But sobriety would come crawling back; it always did. He would look in the mirror and his lips would droop into a shaky frown and his swollen eyes would squint yet again with unmistakable sadness.

For the remainder of those Sundays, he would fight the temptation to get up from the couch. He would lose himself in daytime programming and small mid-day amusements such as watching his pet turtle, Speedy, continuously try to climb up the glass wall of his enclosure, only to fall upon his back and struggle to flip himself back over.

× × ×

Billy's grandmother was taking down her pills like a champ, with what looked like chocolate milk in a Styrofoam cup. Billy picked up the pill cup from her lap with an almost preprogrammed mechanical desire to find something, but alas, it was empty and his early afternoon sobriety rolled on.

Her eyes started to trail and her voice sounded groggy when she called him George and asked him for a cigarette.

"Grandma, it's me, Billy. When did you start smoking?"

Billy looked up at an orderly who was listening in on their conversation. The orderly's name tag read: Shirley.

Billy mouthed to her: "cig-ar-ette?"

"Grace, sugar, you don't smoke," Shirley said, tapping Grandma on the shoulder.

"I want my cigarettes."

Shirley looked at Billy and shook her head with pursed lips. Billy had a vision of Shirley giving Grandma cigarettes on the down-low. *Did Shirley make a secret agreement with Grandma that if she behaved and took her pills like a good little girl that she would be rewarded with cigarettes? Or is Grandma making the whole thing up and just forgot that she doesn't smoke? Her breath didn't smell of cigarettes. Her room didn't have the stench of cigarettes. Did she used to smoke cigarettes and was just always able to hide the truth from you? Or did she smell the cigarettes on you and some kind of transference occurred?*

Grandma looked at Billy's name tag and read the name.

"Billy!"

"Hi Grandma." He kissed her on the cheek.

She placed her translucent hand on Billy's cheek as he held his lips to her for a few seconds. Her eyes were closed, and she was relishing this human contact.

"How's school, Billy?"

"Grandma, I graduated from Mission Mountain years ago. I've been working in New York City."

He again felt the need to keep this story going, that he was still living in New York, still employed at Cobin-Haskett, not in the middle of some escape act, or rescue mission, or something somewhere in between.

"New York City! You have to work real hard, and you have to treat people with respect. People in New York are so rude. You should go back to school. You can never get enough education."

Billy had considered it on a few occasions, had once even enrolled in a chemistry course at LaGuardia Community College after learning Cobin-Haskett would cover tuition costs, but he quit after just one day in the classroom. His cousin, Greg, however, had taken his grandmother's advice to heart. But Greg never needed any guidance. He was George's son, destined to succeed. And Grandma played a big part in getting Peter to stay at Tompkins High when he tried to drop out. She was a big influence on Alan and Cynthia in getting them to send Billy off to boarding school, to Mission Mountain Prep, after a terrible first year at Tompkins. She did it with the best of intentions, to protect Billy from his father, but also to try to protect his father from himself. One fell swoop. She had already seen the violence play out with her husband. Eventually, the importance of staying in school and the need for education became one of her topics on loop, and she would bring it up four more times during Billy's visit.

"I don't think I'm going down that road again for a while. I'm taking the summer off. Maybe find Dad." And out it came again. It still surprised him to be saying the words. "Yea. I guess…try to retrace his steps since he ran off. Maybe bring him back home to Cynthia."

Half a dozen residents now encircled them, more interested in their conversation than the TV now. Their faces looked anesthetized as they had previously, but Billy considered that underneath the zombie countenance there was a humanity still.

Billy turned back to his grandmother, who had a confused look, with her turkey gobbler neck and wrinkled-as-raisins skin, and then a frown locked upon her face. Perhaps, "Dad" and "ran off" had thrown her a curveball. She looked at Billy's name tag. Then more confusion and fluttering eyes. Quivering lips. Then the waterworks. Billy then realized that he now had to explain to his grandmother about Alan's disappearance, running off with just the clothes on his back, as if it were the first time she had heard it. All the others, lost memories.

He wanted to get more from his grandmother before he left—any news about his father, clues to his whereabouts; another part of him wanted to wait until pill time came around again, in case, just in case, and then when it would happen, perhaps he would watch the scene play out all over again, and feel the pain all over again, because he wanted to feel the pain—but also wanted to pull the drain and wash the pain away.

Gracie talked about "Alan," but the stories, he guessed, weren't actually about his father. They were blended anecdotes that could have been about numerous individuals all wrapped up into one. When a story sounded like it could have actually been about his father, one which seemed to fit his character decently well,

Billy still couldn't be sure that it was his father that his grandmother was speaking of. She would break out at points into her stories with other names, and all of a sudden the stories wouldn't necessarily be about Alan anymore but about her deceased husband, about Peter, about George, about Greg. Family even didn't stick. Even when they were the names of her own children and grandchildren.

In the end, Billy gave up. But when he was leaving, he found Shirley in the hallway and asked if his father had happened to come by to see her.

"Oh yeah he did. How could I forget? It broke my heart."

Shirley explained to Billy that Alan came here to tell her something, but it went right through her: "in one ear and out the other," Shirley said. "She can't retain the details, not anymore anyway. But I heard him saying goodbye forever to her, like he was never going to see her again."

It wasn't the first time Billy considered that Alan ran off to kill himself.

Maybe Grandma just wasn't willing to hear that Dad was saying his last goodbye. Her brain wouldn't allow that piece of information to stick. So it was a memory she chose to disregard willingly. Or all control had already been lost, was already too far gone, the recent past wiped clean, save for brief flashes like flickering remnants of dreams. Did she actually know her husband was dead, that he had died more than twenty years ago? Did she still

THE ESCAPIST

consider her family her family or was "family" just another term devoid of meaning—the extinction of day by previous day by previous days, occurring at an exponential rate.

When Billy was still sitting in the room with Gracie and she was in the middle of a possibly true possibly not true story, she stopped talking, fell silent, turned away from him, and started weeping again. That was the end of the story she was telling—it was dead even before it started—but now there was a much more poignant story being told through what he was seeing. Billy considered that she was weeping because she knew how much was gone, was acutely aware of her condition in that moment, and that that was the cause of her breakdown. He considered that perhaps she was reliving some terrible day, or some terrible moment, from her past. He considered that she just needed to cry because of how hard it is to bear the reality of the world. He couldn't quite figure it out—it's tough to get a straight read on someone with Alzheimer's—but it made him quite sad because it made him think about how loved ones someday die and how you have to mourn them, and that you have to mourn even those you thought you didn't love. It made him think about how he could end up like his grandmother too and get sucked into a vortex of having to mourn over and over and over again until forgetting what it even means to mourn. Until forgetting the word "mourn" itself. Until forgetting what any word transcribed to any feeling was. Until there was no feeling at all. And then, maybe, hopefully, peace.

It made him think about his father and about what mourning him would feel like. It made him wonder if his own mourning process had already begun. If it had been transpiring for years. *Why do we only mourn the dead? Do we mourn for those that only feel dead to us? Do we mourn for those that we wished were dead?*

Billy collected his driver's license from the front desk. He headed back up east toward Baltimore, made another loop around Dundalk and didn't stop to see Cynthia for a second time. But seeing the house again made him picture his brother as a boy. *Peter'll have answers. He always did. Let's see what he has to say now. No. Just keep driving in the direction of forward.*

Billy's eyes kept drawing over to the cooler at the floor of the passenger seat, and finally, swiftly, he opened it and reached in with one hand while he kept the other on the wheel. After tossing the towel and a few water bottles onto the passenger seat, he shuffled around until he found the muscle relaxants. He popped open the bottle and poured the pills out into his hand, threw two of them down his throat. He reached into another bottle for the plastic bag that had his psilocybin caps. His eyes were darting from the road to the bag to the road and back. He put a few smallish caps into his mouth and methodically chewed the stale bits down to mush before washing it back.

3

Billy stopped at Ludlow Plaza where he took a piss and bought cigarettes. Billy had been driving for only an hour and his head was already spinning. A memory entered his brain. Still mindful of Felix, he took out his journal and walked to a picnic bench at the highway rest stop.

Instead of mailing Cynthia's meds to her, you decided to hand deliver them. But really you wanted to see him. To stick your hand back into the flame. You made the drive after work. When you got there, the door to the house was open so you just went in. Yelled for Dad. No response. Walked down the hallway, where the bathroom door was slightly open, dim light overhead. He was in the bathtub with his clothes on. He had a washcloth in his hand. He was rubbing his forehead maniacally as if it were a big callused piece of skin. Groaning, small hiccups of anger from his lips. At least he took his shoes off.

You put the meds on the counter and left.

Billy stared into the sky then hopped off the picnic bench. On the road was where he felt he needed to be. He circled around the parking lot in between the semi-trucks and the RVs. He walked past the gas station pumps peering into the cars whose tanks were getting filled to look at lives he knew would never be his.

He got back onto the highway, and it wasn't long before he fell into his clouds of thought, his ponderous state; it was expected—he would typically fall into it when small-dosing on psilocybin. The last time he went big with psilocybin he didn't speak for days with any other living being except for Speedy, the turtle. He wasn't sure what form the clouds would take with this exact quantity of the hallucinogen. And he had left the turtle behind.

But as expected, the world was expanding with the sun fading, the dark coming. The highway's shoulder sped by him, looking right back, acknowledging his solitude. Billy had compassion for the passive, unaccompanied highway. He reached into the cooler, deciding to up his dosage. Ten minutes later he upped it again with another two caps. He wanted a more fruitful journey.

He was driving on cruise control on an empty highway. Fog arose around the two of them, the highway and himself, and he surrendered to the denseness. In doing so, he fell even deeper into a haze. The sounds of the songs from the radio were first rattling the process then blended in, with his seat and his car and the wheels and the road.

Billy was inhaling and exhaling heavily but in a patterned rhythm. An image of his mother appeared, dominating the many other thoughts. Corinth was just as beautiful as she had always been in the pictures, even more beautiful because she now seemed alive, and he repeated the words of her love letter out loud, a letter she had written to an unborn child. The words were sounded out in a woman's voice, the voice of what he knew her voice would sound like.

It was a confession letter, but Corinth had withheld certain truths. She was confessing how hard life can be, yes, and that she and Alan would support him through the tough times, but she never hinted at what those tough times might be. He wanted to omit the line that included Alan's name, but then it wouldn't be staying true to the letter and he had to stay true to the letter; he had to stay true to her. But the line sometimes led to the bad thoughts weaving their way in, now too, and her death became something different, for now he was ripping an imaginary letter to pieces, ripping the image of her to pieces, blaming her and attacking her because it was her fault, and he literally felt his father strangling him. He needed to strangle the life out of him first. *Think of the letter, repeat the words;* back to the letter, back to the sweetest words ever addressed to him. He thought about how she had written it for him, for a person that wasn't even a person yet, just an idea of a person that had weeks to go until tasting the pungent air of the world. But she had written it for herself, too, he knew, so her emotions could be freed. William, she had named him, after her late father.

Billy took out a cigarette and lit it and sucked the smoke into his body, digesting it, gulping the flavor, felt it buzzing his bones and settling his ill-at-ease nerves while navigating through the clouds. His mind continued to drift to different ideas. Next, the image of a drawbridge. It was medieval, shimmering like a lighthouse for ships lost at sea. The image entered then left then entered again until it was stationary in his line of sight; it was directly up ahead, and he kept driving toward it, yet as soon as he thought he was getting closer to it, it would then seem farther away. It was suddenly his desired destination, yet the more he drove toward it, the farther away it became, as if it were racing away from him at a slightly faster speed than he could maintain. He sped up, but the image in the distance sped up too, and if only he could just get to it.

He looked down to the passenger seat and to the cooler on the passenger seat floor to take inventory of the items he would need for the excursion: *snacks—check, canisters of water—check, cigarettes—check, pot for balance—check, and ear swabs—check. Ear swabs, yes. Ear swabs to prevent the blood from dripping onto your shirt when the speed comes close to that of light; goggles, too. Goggles to protect your eyes in case the windshield splintered. And a white Nascar racing bodysuit in the back. The bodysuit for any other faulty ill-equipped, badly manufactured piece of the Nissan that could happen to combust during your passing.*

It wouldn't be long now, he felt, until he would hit his destined drawbridge, even though it continued to be elusive. There he would penetrate time.

✕ ✕ ✕

The moving picture show through the windshield was getting dimmer and dimmer and harder to see. He pulled off the highway at Whitney Point and into an embankment.

A reoccurring vision transpired: a surreal picture, one of simplicity, of minimalism, a clean beguiling circumstance; he was now in a placid park, envisioning his brother and himself on a merry-go-round, Peter forever at his side. When he snapped back, his heart was beating hard, and he was sweaty. He stumbled out of his car to stretch out his cramped body. He took a piss then got back in the Nissan. He popped down the sun visor and looked in the mirror. His reflection was tired, big bags under the eyes. A ghostly complexion. The beginnings of a beard. He began a debate with his reflection:

Tired. Tired of running!

"Why do you think we're writing this shit down, asshole?" his reflection said back to him. "We're confronting it now."

But, still running.

"Running yes. But now we're running right for it. We aren't running away anymore. We're taking a stand. No more running from emotions! We are driving to find him."

Billy needed a shower. He needed something, some sort of release; his eyes got an odd twitch and the inside tips of his brows pointed downward, his left brow slightly further down than his right. He suddenly realized that his thoughts had overwhelmed him. "Write it down."

And so he tried. But navigating through this hallucination where time was malleable was proving difficult, yet he was still grasping at something interesting as these eccentric notions continued to pour out of his pen, something tangible, and it was that even if he were able to go back to the way it was, get a second chance, in this scenario, he still wouldn't be able to forget what had already occurred. Like going back to elementary school with the accumulated knowledge you had attained many years later—there's no redo, only replay. He still had time, he thought, until he hit his drawbridge.

The endeavor to write, however, was short-lived. It was too cloudy to concentrate. He decided that just driving, just going, was better than sitting still. He smoked a bowl then put on his white and black bandana to hold his oily hair in place.

The yellow lines painted past him. The side scenery melted away. He was getting closer to his goal, he felt. The clouds of thought, though, had gotten to a new high. Staring at the same black lonely road, it seemed to control him. Time was fast, then slow. When things seemed clear and unconfined with the dopamine taken in in larger doses, the planet felt bigger with a slower click of the clock, but when life got hazy again, the world was imploding and the minute hand circled like the second hand.

He became so anxious that he made his mind slow down, slowed down his breathing, and in doing so, slowed down the car because all was connected. He kept singing *Street Spirit* to himself, a Radiohead song that was ingrained in his memory from his youth:

Rows of houses, all bearing down on me
I can feel their blue hands touching me
All these things in all positions
All these things will one day take control
And fade out again, and fade out
This machine will, will not communicate
These thoughts and the strain I am under
Be a world child, form a circle
Before we all, go under
And fade out again, and fade out again

The bombarding thoughts quieted.

THE ESCAPIST

Immerse your soul in love, Immerse your soul in love
Immerse your soul in love, Immerse your soul in love
Immerse your soul in love, Immerse your soul in love

He continued to sing it, over and over again with no one to hear. He yelled it, yelled it so loud that it hurt his throat. But he liked it, it was his voice. He continued to sing, yet it got softer and softer as he kept on singing, and as time passed, it became a whisper and was just repeating itself, as if his brain were not telling his voice to do it, as if it had become some sort of thought-muting auto-mechanism, an instinctual act. His legs ached. He pulled off at the Bastillo Mall exit, into the mall parking lot and shut his eyes. His vision was dismal but satisfying, and simple. With Peter by his side, his whole body suddenly eased.

There was no way to know how much time had passed. It felt like hours but could have been mere minutes. He popped down the sun visor to look again at his reflection. He saw the face, eyes dilated, hair unkempt. He asked it question after question, demeaning it, giving it judging glances as a teacher would her unruly student.

His badgering of himself was quickly interrupted by flashes of blue and red shimmering in the mirror. He then fixed his eyes on what was flashing behind him. He saw a police car, then another, then another, then two more quickly approaching.

Yet the flashing lights sped right past his car, never even slowed down; they weren't coming to get him for they had some other emergency to attend to, but they remained for Billy, and their phantasms had now made a semicircle around his car, blocking him in. As if performing an avant-garde dance, he slipped the imaginary bodysuit onto his body, placed the imaginary goggles over his face and slid the imaginary swabs of cotton into his ear cavities. He got out of the car slowly. As he stood up, he stretched his legs and his back and stared at a volcano of lights of blue and red and neon all the while humming his song. *Immerse your soul in love. Immerse your soul in love. Immerse your soul in love.* Out of the flashing lights grew the phantom officers that were now slyly approaching the Nissan. He smiled at the blue and black and see-through officers. He opened his palms and extended his arms outward. His right hand clasped closed except for his pointer finger, which he stuck out and waved around at the armed officers.

Though his Nissan was old, it still had the same spunk that it had at its initial run, and he sped up quickly so that the drawbridge was now coming closer to him, finally, closer and closer, for it was now coming to embrace him. He was speeding, and the world outside of his car was pulsating and breathing, and the shadow of his drawbridge came over him and the Nissan.

He was feeling a sense of accomplishment, victory. The haze was swirling, but it was radiant and affirmative now, and this kind of excitement, this kind of raw adrenalin, was enough for him to consider not changing anything when he went back in time, not one thing, just so he could experience for a second time such a thrill. But as his car was barreling onto the drawbridge and he was feeling its kinetic energy morphing his body, one memory was flickering, one sudden moment of clarity in an otherwise paralyzing intoxication—he was being beaten and raped, and even though he was numb to it at the time, he was feeling it now, and it hurt. He was screaming in agony as his Nissan was suddenly ablaze with flames of bright red and blue with smoke billowing and stroboscopic bolts of color intensifying. He was now back in time, but in this moment he was now attacking the offender, his father, before the offender, his father, could attack him, making Billy not the victim but the victimizer.

4

The swooshing of cars passing by were the first sounds he heard. With his face planted against the driver's side window, he listened listlessly to the harmonic wave of tires on pavement. His mind went to sitting in science class at Mission Mountain and the large Ms. Broder running back and forth in the classroom with a piano tuner to teach her students about the Doppler Effect, her breasts jiggling in the process for the class's amusement.

He opened his eyes. His car was ten or so feet from the side of a back road, parked crookedly on grass, car key still in the ignition. He got out into the early morning chill where the grass was wet with mildew. His eyes were bloodshot, and his belly grumbling. He peered off into the trees, down past a ravine and saw a small town center in the distance. He got back into the car, looked around and saw his things strewn about the seats and floors. He contemplated what he had turned himself into the night before. The nonexistent drawbridge.

He pulled into a gas station to fill his tank and then went in to buy coffee along with a few donuts. He asked the attendant where he was, and the attendant told him he was in Bastillo.

"Bastillo, where?"

"You're in Maryland, guy."

"Right, right."

"Where you from?"

"From the west coast," he lied, without considering why. "Here visiting family."

"Good for you, guy. You have family in Bastillo? Or family in Baltimore?"

"Virginia Beach, actually, just passing through. You guys sell maps?"

The attendant pointed to a shelf behind the counter. Billy got a regional map of Maryland, Virginia, and West Virginia.

Back in the car, he took out the map to find a good route to Virginia Beach. Instead of taking I-95, he decided to take some of the smaller roads and highways that drove along the water. He wanted to be close to it.

✕ ✕ ✕

There was a National Cheerleading competition in Virginia Beach that weekend. The girls were everywhere, with their skimpy uniforms, hair braided perfectly and smiles ear to ear. The enthusiastic parents were what bothered Billy the most. They carried around flags that displayed the names of their daughters' cheerleading squads. Their cars were chalked up with corny expressions and words of encouragement. They bickered and sneered when walking past one another on street corners—lots of loud, seemingly pointless cheering. Billy's first night there he found a cheap restaurant with outdoor seating overlooking the ocean. He had a craving for a crab cake sandwich. He wanted to have quiet with his meal, but the whoop-whooping emanating from the mouths of the cheerleaders and their families made that impossible.

He found a hostel on the outskirts of town, checked in and plopped his belongings on top of his bed. He'd left the cooler and his other belongings in the car. An old fat man with tattoos ran the establishment. He was wearing a green patrol hat that said USAF Vietnam Vet. He asked Billy if he wanted to hang that evening, play some cards. Billy said he had plans—he sat in his car and chain-smoked with the windows down, smelling the salt air.

The next morning Billy woke early and found Peter's address on a scrap paper in his wallet. He knew his brother shared a small shack close to the water with some of his army friends; he had given him his address the last time they talked on the phone. It was back when he was still working at Cobin-Haskett. Billy had called to talk to him about Alan's disappearance. He had only found out about it when Cynthia had called him a few days before that, and she mentioned it in passing, that Alan had left her in the middle of the night and hadn't come back, but Billy knew that Cynthia was really calling to ask him to send her some more meds. That Lithium Carbonate, that Alprazolam, that Xanax. More Quetiapine. She had over time tapered off all the Aripiprazole, Venlafaxine, Trazodone. But she knew her meds like he did and knew when certain ones needed revisiting. He ended the call with her as quickly as he could, saying that he would get them and mail them out to her the next time he had access to the pharm.

Billy hoped that Peter would know more about Alan's whereabouts. Could at least give him better guidance about it. But he also just wanted to see Peter. It had been so long since their last fight. Peter never liked speaking about Alan to others. Neither did Billy. Even just between the two of them, the topic of their father was hardly ever brought up. When Billy broached the subject, Peter would be quick to change it. And when they had talked on the phone, Peter did it again—abruptly started talking about the *Fast and the Furious* movie he was in the middle of watching, something about Dodge Chargers. But he did tell Billy to come visit some time, not actually thinking that his brother would be showing up at his doorstep.

Billy walked along the beach and through some

small back roads to get to Peter's house. He passed an outdoor book vendor and on a whim, purchased two books that caught his eye: *Astral Voyages; Mastering the Art of Interdimensional Travel* by Dr. Bruce Goldberg and *Moon Palace* by Brooklyn writer Paul Auster. When he arrived at his brother's, he saw someone sunbathing in the backyard watching past the fence the procession of beautiful young women strolling along the beach.

"Hey Peter, is that you?"

"Yea? Who dat?"

"Peter, it's me."

"Who's me?"

"It's me, dude, Billy."

"Billy. What? Little Shrimp! Mi amigo! What the fuck are you doing here? Now's not a good time, Little Shrimp. No, it's ok. Come over here! Let me get a look at you."

Billy approached and stood over his brother blocking the sun. The sunrays radiated around him giving him an almost angelic aura. Peter gracelessly got himself out of the sunken seat of the lawn chair and faced his brother. "Wow. You look like shit. You look worse every time I see you."

"You look like shit too."

They walked inside. His house was empty and looked as though he was just moving in or out. There was a lack of furniture, no wall decorations, poor lighting. There were more guys in the house, one cruising around in his bathrobe; the rest had their shirts off, some with monstrous tattoos. Peter had a rather large belly and big beard with long hair draping to his chin, also all tatted up. A lot of it was fresh ink.

"Why are you here? For the cheerleaders? Lots of eye candy around here right now."

They were standing in the kitchen on either side of the island.

"Mmm, yes, high school girls."

"You gotta try not to think about their age. Just appreciate their beauty. It's as good as it gets. God's greatest creation. The young cheerleader. I'm going to head over with my man to see some of the dance routines later today. You should come with. Who knows, you may even meet a little honey to sink your teeth into."

"I'm kinda seeing someone right now."

"She don't got to know about it."

"I don't cheat," Billy said sternly, "…unlike you and Dad."

"Dude, you just fucking got here. Already talking shit. You come here just to give me shit?"

"No."

"And you're already bringing him up. Let's at least have a few drinks first."

"Well then give me a fucking drink."

"Man, why you want to bring him up. You really want to talk about him right now?"

"That's why I'm here."

"Well, I don't want to."

"Fine. Anyway, I was just saying."

"Just saying what."

"Just saying, I don't cheat."

"Good for you, fucker—you're a model American. Here's your medal."

Billy turned directions and looked around the house. "Forget it. Can I use your shower? I haven't washed in days."

"Yea, fine. You need a towel?"

"Yea! You want me to air dry?"

"Upstairs, there's a towel in the closet by the bathroom. Can't guarantee it's clean. Bathroom is at the end of the hall. Don't fuck with anything."

Billy turned on the water and got in. There was only a little stick of soap in the tub, something that was once a bar. He turned the nozzle until the water was steaming. He liked it hot. He stood and just let the water run over him for a while, through him, to warm his blood. It was one of the only times that he felt he could be free from all of it. Being in water. It was the most natural of remedies.

The bathroom door opened.

"Little Shrimp."

It was Peter.

"You and I both know Dad loved the fuck out of Cynthia. You can't tell me he didn't love her. Cause he did…and…and while I was off trying to find prostitution rings in Fallujah and contract venereal diseases, you know what he was doing? He was bunked away writing her love letters. He showed me a letter once. He may have cheated on her, but that was a different dad. He was a changed man over there—not like he was back then, not like before. She was the most important thing in the world to him."

"Until he got back home."

"All I know is that when we saw each other over there, he talked about her constantly, how much he needed her, how much he missed her. Carried her picture in his pocket. She's probably the reason that he made it back here alive, in one piece."

"Physically in one piece."

"You know, I gotta stop. I gotta get a drink. It's just, it's difficult for me to talk about it right at this moment. What happened to Dad. Seeing him like that fucked me up. I'm still not right. And you know I got problems of my own."

Billy turned the shower nozzle off. He could hear Peter snorting something and wiping his nose. Suddenly, Billy hungered for his bed back in New York. For the big city wails, thrums, and dreams. He had thought he was ready for this adventure. He'd thought he was a man.

Billy got dressed in the same clothes he had been wearing and went downstairs. Peter was finishing off a shot. He put a comforting hand around the back of

Billy's neck with a slap and then swung a playful but firm fist to Billy's belly. Billy toppled over.

"Get on up. I'm gonna shower too. Relax with Phillipo over there. Phillipo! Make my brother a drink! Then we gonna go check out some cheerleaders."

Tickets were $35 a piece. Billy never would have coughed up that much money to see cheerleaders do their team routines, but Peter paid for his ticket. They sat in the bleachers behind all the parents and family members. Phillipo came with them. They may have been the only onlookers not in one way or another related to the participants besides some of the horny high school Virginia Beach boys scattered about. The Fayetteville Jaguars were finishing up their number when the three sat down. The music was loud and obnoxious. The troupe concluded with a few lavish tosses of bodies, and then they all suddenly dropped to the floor with their legs split and their right arms in the air, their pointer fingers pointed to the sky. Smiles were painted onto every face, their guts puffing in and out from exhaustion. Everyone clapped, including Peter and Phillipo, and the girls ran off on their tippy toes with perfectly arched backs, their fingers wiggling in the air until they were off the court.

"I saw Grandma," Billy told Peter over the noise of

the crowd. "I saw her before I made my way to you. She can't remember much, but the love in her heart…it's still there…that won't fade."

"I got some stories about her, losing her mind and shit, if you want me to tell them. But that's good though. We shouldn't shatter the image you got of her."

"Yea, she enforced the law pretty hard, I know it. You know it. She was the real deal. But she always wanted the best for us. It's fucked how she is right now."

"She had a Bubba too, bro."

"What?"

"Bubba, dude. She and Grandpa had one too that they used on Dad. Found out about it over Christmas."

Peter hardly ever talked about Bubba, and Billy thought it was weird that Peter was actually bringing it up. If only Peter knew that Bubba was here, in Virginia Beach, just a few miles away, in Billy's car.

Bubba, of course, was the name they coined for the cane Alan used on them—a skinny walking stick carved into the shape of a serpent. When Billy moved to New York City, it was one of the few objects he took with him from the old family duplex in Baltimore, and when Billy was packing up to leave New York to head to Felix's farm, he decided that it would serve as his walking stick for any necessary long hikes or walking expeditions. For all that time in New York it had just sat in his closet, forgotten.

"So, how long are you planning on staying here? Or…

what are you doing here, for real?"

"I have some ideas. Nothing solid. Nothing set in stone. I know some places he's always wanted to go. Places he's already been."

"You tracking him down?"

"I don't know. I think so."

"Like finding a needle in a haystack, Shrimp. You may as well go home and save yourself the money. Tell me about this girl you're seeing."

"Her name's Nicole, she—" Before Billy could continue, the lights dimmed and an electric drum and bass beat kicked into gear. The girls of Upper Marlboro came charging out in a V-shaped procession. They stood stock still in the same V-lineup with their heads facing the ground and their arms at their sides, their hands clenched into fists. The drum and bass beat picked up in tempo and came at them faster and faster until it was one steady break of sound. Then it stopped and the blue and green and yellow lights flashed on as an electronic-techno remix of a Justin Timberlake song blasted out of the speakers, and the girls were off—flipping and dancing in unison.

"Her name is Nicole," Billy yelled over the music. "She's a flight attendant. She said that she's going to try to meet me wherever I end up. Her flights could very well line up with…well…wherever it is I'm fucking going."

"That's good. Anything to help you to take your mind

off finding him. I don't know what you're trying to gain from this little detective mission of yours. Did you ever consider that he doesn't want to be found?"

"There's something you're not telling me, Peter," Billy yelled, staring coldly at his brother's face, at his ruffled beard with the willy-nilly mustache hairs sprouting over the sides of his mouth, his two front teeth still peeking out through his lips as they always had.

"After the show."

5

Toward the end of Billy's tenure at Cobin-Haskett, the basement mailroom became a dreadful hideout where he would lock himself away, only coming out to make his daily delivery runs, always lost in his thoughts with a hatred for himself that was growing. He was able to successfully float by in this corporate world, moving up the corporate mailroom ladder from Clerk 1 to Clerical Specialist within just a couple of months. This corporate mobility came effortlessly to him—he was simply doing the tasks assigned to him, nothing more, nothing less. After work, Billy would go back to his apartment and stay there for the evening ritual. His depression during some of those stretches in New York made him feel utterly ruined. His only respite came from heavier drug intake, larger mixed batches of uppers, downers, mindbenders and painkillers, along with his tried and true constants, his anti-anxiety/

depression pills, his muscle relaxants, his amphetamines, and more and more cannabis. He was smoking before work, during his lunch break and often while doing trash disposal in the back alleyway.

One Friday when the workday was coming to a close, Billy decided to not go home for the ritual and instead to walk the streets. He snorted some coke up his nose in the bathroom before leaving. On his way out he saluted his supervisor goodbye, still working away at the distribution table, who said "okeey" to him in a clearly derisive tone before dropping his gaze back down to his work. Billy flashed a fake smile and exited the building. He walked down Park Avenue with Grand Central Station and the MetLife building in view. He came to the underpass at Grand Central a few minutes later and walked through it and over to Vanderbilt Avenue where he was approaching a blond-haired woman standing outside of Rothman's Irish Pub smoking a cigarette. This is how he met Nicole.

"Can I bum one of those off you?" he asked without hesitation. She was many years older than he was and had crow's feet crinkling around her eyes, hair that was starting to thin, but the most beautiful cheeks he had ever seen. Her skin looked as if it were glowing, and it was that which he had always loved about her. It was just a request for a cigarette, a simple request, no harm, no foul.

"Sure," she said.

"Here, let me give you a dollar for it. Here, take it. Take it. No? Are you sure? You positive? Thank you so much. Thanks a lot. I appreciate it. I'm Billy, by the way."

"Hi Billy, I'm Nicole."

"Hey Nicole. So what do you do?" The words were coming out of him easily and hastily. The cocaine.

"I'm a trolley trollop."

"A trolley trollop?"

"Yea…a coffee jockey, a tart with a cart."

"A what?"

"A pilot nanny. A flight comfort engineer."

"I'm lost."

"Christ. I'm a fucking flight attendant."

"Oh, that's cool. Funny. Ha. *Ha!* So, do you like what you do?"

"What do you think?"

"Anyway, what're you up to tonight, Nicole?"

"Just hanging with my girlfriends."

"I work in publishing."

"Oh."

"Yea."

"Good for you." Nicole lit up a new cigarette with the one she had just finished.

"Me too?" Billy had already sucked half of his cigarette down.

"Why not." She gave Billy a new one, and he followed Nicole's lead moments later by lighting his the same way.

"So where do you live, Nicole?"

"I live in western New York, just here in the city for the night. I'm always traveling for work, obviously, but find myself in New York City quite often."

"Yea, well, I'm a pretty successful guy. I live on 67th street. Central Park's my backyard. You should come to one of my parties next time you're in the city."

Nicole didn't respond, just kept smoking down her cigarette.

"Though the apartment is really nice, it makes me feel empty to be there by myself with no girlfriend, no television, just tons of books and a stereo system. Just all this open space, huge windows. Late at night I sometimes put my book down and simply stare up at the ceiling which seems miles away, and I…I…bah…bah." Billy kept making some strange noises and speaking a little more gibberish as he lost his train of thought but wanted to keep speaking, wanted these lies to keep coming out of his mouth.

Lying to a complete stranger was actually making him feel better. He was trying to make her think highly of him because, for that short-lived moment, it increased his self-worth. This was not a new occurrence—he found himself lying to people a lot, mostly complete strangers like Nicole, and the lies came out of him quickly and naturally, and it would be to a similar effect—after he would tell a fib, a few minutes later, later that day or that night when by himself with the opportunity to reflect, it would always have the opposite result and make him feel even worse. It was just like any of his other addictions. When his self-esteem would begin to spiral back down, he would end up regressing right back to his old ways of self-embellishment and deceit. The next person that would meet him would not be meeting him but meeting a different self, one more accomplished and confident and gifted, because when he stepped into those shoes, they became so comfortable, but every night before getting into bed, those shoes had to come off.

Only a minute had passed and he realized what he had done—what his brain was up to again. He looked at her short and stocky figure, glanced away into the street and then back at her and then away again. He shook his head.

"What is your deal?" Nicole asked.

"I'm sorry. I'm going to be honest with you. I was just lying. About everything. I do that sometimes. I'm actually just a waste of space. A no-talent nothing. I live in a basement apartment in a shitty neighborhood in Queens and sort mail for a living. I'm sorry for wasting your time."

Billy turned to walk away.

"Hold up a second," Nicole said.

Billy turned around.

"Come here." She held out her hands. She wiggled her fingers motioning for him to come to her. He took her up on it. They hugged.

"That was…unexpected."

"It seemed like you needed it."
"Thank you."
"Come in and get a drink with me."
"Okay."

In the morning, lying half awake in her hotel room bed, he watched as she was getting dressed, and Billy asked her to be his girlfriend. After all, she was willing to sleep with him, and he loved her skin.

"Be your girlfriend? You're kidding, right?"

"No, why don't we be boyfriend-girlfriend? Like, going steady."

"You're cute," she said.

"So what do you say?"

"Sure thing, kid." She wrote down her phone number on the hotel stationary, bent over, which exposed her cleavage, and gave him a kiss and a smile, then he watched her as she walked out the door.

Funny thing—after that, they maintained a relationship. They talked on the phone almost every other night. They shared stories about work, her mundane flights and his mundane mail sorting. She told him about her upbringing in a small town called Williamson, just south of Lake Ontario in western New York, about her deceased parents, about her uncle Felix who raised her on his big seventy acre farm after her parents died. She described Felix as being quite a character. She talked about what it was like growing up as a farm girl in such a beautiful place, surrounded by manicured fields and farm animals, what it was like growing up without parents. She told him about how she got into being a flight attendant, how she wanted to see the world. Billy didn't tell her much about his upbringing, mostly that it was shitty and not worth going into. He just told her that he came from a military family, was raised by his father and stepmother in Baltimore, had an older brother, and that his mother died when he was a baby. She asked him how his mother died, and he told her that she had been sick for a long time. He didn't tell her what the real illness was, didn't tell her about how his brother found her in the bathtub.

It was exactly three weeks after they had first met that Billy got the call from Cynthia telling him about how his father had run off in the middle of the night. Nicole called him a few hours later, and he didn't pick up, instead performing his ritual. It was the first time he let her call go unanswered. He didn't answer the following night either. But the night after that, sitting on his couch peering down at freshly notated sticky notes on the coffee table, he swiftly picked up his phone and gave her a ring.

"I don't know what I'm even doing at work anymore," he said to her. "Shit sucks. My apartment sucks. There is nothing for me here. I can't afford anything. And it's just…lonely—millions of people everywhere, all walking around with their blinders on. When are you coming back?"

"I have to check my schedule. Not sure. It'll be soon though, I promise."

"Listen," Billy said after a pause, "there's something I wanted to bring up with you. Something I wanted to ask you. I'm feeling kinda miserable these days. You know how I am. I'm hot and then I'm cold, I have these highs and lows, the highs being miserable and the lows being even more miserable."

"It's really that bad? It doesn't seem that bad."

"It is."

"Well, why don't you make a change?"

"That's actually what I wanted to talk to you about."

"What kind of change?"

"Well…I was thinking about going somewhere else."

"Going where?"

"Well, I was thinking maybe, maybe I could spend some time with your uncle Felix. You told me all about the big farm he operates. How he's always looking for workers around the property. And it's kinda close to where you live, too. We'd only be like twenty-minutes apart. I could see you more that way when you're in town from work. Maybe he could set me up with a place to stay or something. Working in the sun could do me some good. Some good old-fashioned exercise."

"It's funny, I was just talking to him about you. He is actually looking for more groundskeepers. He said he needs someone he can trust. He could probably take you on. And I trust you, Billy. Let me call him."

Nicole called back a few minutes later and had Billy call Felix to introduce himself and get some more information. They talked for fifteen minutes before Felix offered him the job. Billy had always been articulate, always had a certain way with words. It attracted people to him. The job would be as a groundskeeper at Brevard Farm, with its seventy acre range. Felix told him that he occupied it by his lonesome but constantly had workers roaming around. He told him that it was a thriving place, a beautiful paradise. By the time they hung up, Billy was already in a kind of mania and started making the necessary preparations in his head. He sorted out his drugs, counting quantities and marking down the tallies on sticky notes, gathering details for a necessary restock before departing. He called his pharma-connects. Two made deliveries to his apartment a few hours later, another he had to meet on the street the next day—Billy got in his car and they drove around the block while doing the exchange. He knew he would need to see his psychiatrist to refill his prescriptions. He wouldn't tell him about his plans for leaving the city. He had already mentally disengaged from his current existence. It took no time at all.

Billy, Peter, and Phillipo left halfway through the cheer-leading competition. Peter could tell Billy was bored and wasn't paying much attention to the attractive specimens. They walked over to one of Peter's neighborhood pubs. He bought the three of them whiskeys, neat, and Bud Lights as chasers.

"Let's talk Peter. For real. Please, tell me what I want to know."

"Honestly, Little Shrimp, I don't know how comfortable I feel talking to you about this. I went through it too, man. Phillipo, too. Phillipo, you want to talk about it?"

"Nah, man. I want to forget about it, actually."

"Yea, forget about it, Shrimp."

"Sometimes it's good for people to talk about things," Billy said. "I just want to see him. I want to talk to him."

"I get that. But you have to recognize that sometimes people need to just start over again. Be on their own. And he didn't want to start doping again, either. If he's on the move maybe he ain't doping. And you're staying clean?"

"Clean as a whistle."

"Good," Peter said, nodding his head. "But you still helping Cynthia out with her meds, right?"

"Yea."

"Ok. Good."

"So why aren't you on the move, too?"

"Are you kidding? I ran the fuck away. Moved to Virginia Beach where no one could find me."

"I found you."

"Yea, you did. But I gave you my address."

"Where is he, Peter."

"I can't say."

"Peter."

He shook his head. Billy repeated his question. He received the same cold shaking of the head. Sweat had begun to develop on Billy's forehead. A vein pulsated above his eye. Billy brashly reached over the table and grabbed Peter's shirt collar and pulled him close. This behavior sprung out of him so suddenly, yet he wasn't surprised by it.

"Where the fuck is he, man! Tell me where the fuck he is, Pete!" Billy pulled Peter even closer to his face and with a cracked voice continued: "I am going to find him—and you are going to tell me where he is. Right now."

Peter maneuvered out of his seat and shimmied around the table, all while Billy's hands were still clenched around his collar, and Phillipo was snickering in between them. When Peter was close enough, he grabbed Billy's arms and slowly twisted his body around, forcing Billy to lose his grip and his momentum. Billy headbutted the air until Peter engaged him in a headlock; Peter lifted Billy's body into the air by his belt and his neck like he was picking up a saddle to place upon a horse, and then he dropped Billy down to the floor, knocking the wind out of him.

"You think you can interrogate me, Little Shrimp? Is

that it? You think you're better than me?"

"No, I…" he stopped, coughing, fighting for air.

"No, you're not better than me, you're not my superior. You're nothing. You're a piece of shit. So you just relax, Shrimp! Just fucking relax."

Others in the bar had quieted down and were looking on at the commotion in the back where they had been sitting. "Things hunky-dory over there, Pete?" the bartender called over to him.

"Yea, my brother's just being a tool, Scotty." Peter held Billy down by his elbow. "He's chill now—aren't you Little Shrimp?"

Billy nodded. Peter let go of him and sat back down, took a sip of his whisky. Billy's Bud Light had spilled onto the floor and onto his shirt and pants during the abrupt violence.

"Just like Dad. Fucking spazzoid. Short fucking bouts of anger—this aggression, I see where you get it from. You guys belong together."

"Look who's talking," Billy said under his breath.

Billy kept panting heavily and held his chest as his breathing evened out. "I fucking hate you, man," he cried out. "You never had my back. You knew exactly what he was fucking doing to me, and you did fucking nothing. Nothing! And you know it, too."

"Little Shrimp, we're not fucking getting into this again."

"Of course we're not getting into it because you've

never wanted to get into it."

There was silence for a few long seconds until Phillipo broke out into his giggles again.

"Look Shrimp," Peter said over Phillipo's snickering, "the truth is I don't know where he is. He came here, ok. He just stayed the night. One night. Then he moved on. I don't even know if he had a destination in mind. He wants to be alone, Little Shrimp. He doesn't care to see anybody. And that especially includes you, man."

"Where was he heading next? You can at least tell me where he was going next."

"I dropped him off at the bus station. He boarded a bus that was headed for Savannah. That's all I know, Little Shrimp. But Little Shrimp, let it be, man, just let him be."

Billy got up from the bar and left without saying goodbye.

Billy fantasized that seeing Peter this time would be different, that maybe he'd be able to spend the rest of his life with his brother happily by his side, as his equal, that they'd be able to sit together, peacefully, at that placid place to watch the merry-go-round go round and round and round. Stupid.

× × ×

As a kid you used to sometimes crawl into Peter's bed. You would wake him up and jump around the bed, lie on top of him and try to suffocate him. Not for real. You were just testing him. You always used to test him. He tested you, too. It helped. It helped keep you on your toes. You were keeping him on his toes, too, even though he didn't need to be kept on his toes like you. You poked at two moles that protruded out of his neck. You pulled on one of them.

--What are these things anyway?

--They're dabbers.

--What's a dabber?

--It's a growth that forms on your body. It develops and grows over time. The more experience that you have in life, the more dabbers you get.

You played around with it some more and squished it with your fingers.

--Does that hurt?

--Nope.

--How about that?

--Nope.

--What about now?

--Still nothing.

Blood appeared.

--Anything now?

--Nope.

It was as if Peter were immune to pain. A superhero. You showed him the piece of mole you picked off his body.

--Bastard! You just erased five years of my life!

--Sorry, Petey.

--It's ok. I'm still young. There are still a million things for me

to see, a million things for me to get wrapped up in.

If only escaping the past were as simple as ripping off a few moles. He doesn't see it the way you see it. What Dad did. Maybe Peter would still just call it tough love. He wouldn't call it that other thing, but really, that's what it was.

6

You were a little shrimpy piece of shit in middle school—that's what Dad and Peter and Cynthia would call you, Little Shrimp—with big ears that were like open car doors. You were a spazzoid. You were a walking target for assholes like Aaron Pearlman and Chris Mews. Aaron used to grab your ears and yell wizzaard when he passed you in the halls. Chris would sneak up behind you and pull your pants down showing off to many of the gawking onlookers the neon-colored underwear that Grandma had picked out for you months earlier.

In homeroom, they would constantly torment you by leaving notes on your desk before you arrived. One note said: don't look in your desk drawer. Whatever you do, don't look.

So you looked of course...and they were cracking up in the back of the room...and a giant pink dildo was there waiting for you. You couldn't take it out and throw it away because then you would be seen with a giant pink dildo in your hands. You had to wait until the end of the school day after everyone had left in order to dispose of it. But it was hours until the end of the day and until then, that dildo had to remain in the desk drawer. Plenty of time for Chris and Aaron to spread rumors about how you masturbate in the school bathroom with a giant pink dildo. People checked in your desk drawer to see if the rumor was true and there it was, proof of your ill-doing. You didn't tell Grandma or Dad or Peter or even Cynthia that you were picked on. You wanted to keep it to yourself. You didn't want them to know that you were bullied. But eventually Peter got wind of it. He usually had a way of finding out these things, either through his high school friends with younger siblings in middle school, or, through reading your mind. He was always good at that.

Uninvited, Peter and two of his buddies from high school walked into Kipps Middle School. There were no security guards or metal detector then, so they could enter unnoticed. These three mythological creatures, these larger than life heroes, were now walking the halls and making their way to your homeroom. They entered and Mrs. Wickerson gave each of them a smile, light hugs and pats on the back. They weren't her best students by far, but a joy to spend time with: glittering adolescents from days past, back again, paying their respects to a teacher that always had the highest hopes for anyone that had sat in her classroom.

Mrs. Wickerson introduced the three high schoolers, previous Kipps Middle School dwellers. Your classmates looked upon them in awe, Chris and Aaron included. Peter came over to your desk and sat atop, keeping one foot stabilized on the ground, while the other swung freely from side to side.

--What's up, Little Shrimp.

--Peter, what are you doing here?

--Just came by to see some old teachers, is all. And to see my younger bro.

He slapped his hand around the back of your neck and thrust his fist down into the desk of your chair striking your belly and flicking out his fingers at your groin with a soft nippy blow. And then in a hushed voice said to you: now point out those two shitheads for me.

--What two shitheads? you whispered back.

--Don't play stupid with me, Little Shrimp. Now point them out. Do it.

You bashfully turned your head around and just planted a death-stare on Chris and Aaron in the corner of the room. Peter saw who you were looking at. He gave them a cold hard stare too. Peter's two friends looked up from their side conversations with the rest of the class and also planted their slanted eyes on the two troublemakers in the back of the room. Chris and Aaron saw that their eyes were on them now, but they didn't really know what to make of it. You turned back around and faced the front of the room. Peter and his friends did the same. After a few more minutes they said their goodbyes, left the classroom.

The next day, and then the rest of the school year, and after, Chris and Aaron never even looked at you. They were scared shitless of you now. You never asked Peter what he said or what he did. But whatever it was, it worked. Yea, he saved you from them. And yea, he saved you again years later when he was back from Iraq, when he pulled you out of that crack den. But he couldn't save you when it really mattered.

× × ×

Billy closed the journal. He drove back to Peter's house, considered stopping but didn't. He knew what his next destination had to be: Georgia. *Find dad.* He continued straight for the freeway and headed south without a clue of what he'd do once he got there. He was back in the driver's seat, back on the road, back to uninteresting radio and empty highway. Despite having tussled with his brother on the dirty floor of a bar and having beer spilled over him, he was still feeling clean from the shower he had taken that morning—his mind felt clean—but it was something that needed to be eradicated because cleanliness could lead to the darkness.

During his time at Cobin-Haskett, he was showering just about every day, applying an overabundance of deodorant; it aided in masking some animalistic primality and associated urges that he needed to escape from, yet so often felt pulled to return to. When he got a taste for it after a long weekend, an extra long shower, extra soapy bubbles, double rinse-throughs of shampoo and conditioner were in order. Yet, the darkness would wash over. Taking the job at the farm, working in the dirt, smelling of something more ripe, was partly that pull taking over to return to that primal place. It rightly started after having been offered the job at the farm. Even before he put in his two-week notice at Cobin-

Haskett, he stopped showering; he allowed his body to get dirty, his head to get dirty, to stay dirty. After he put in his two weeks, his dirtiness was apparent; it was apparent in his odor, in his greasy hair, in his unshaven face, in the bags under his eyes, in his callousness.

His supervisor told him to leave after three days. His supervisor said that he already had someone that was willing and able to fill in for him. Billy asked who it was. His supervisor said that it wasn't important. Billy asked why it wasn't important. His supervisor rolled his eyes and then upstretched his head as if to ask God "why me?" and then retorted: "We're giving the job to Phil."

"Phil! Phil's handicapped! How's he going to work the floors!"

"Phil's been here a long time. He deserves it," and then after a pause, "he deserves it a lot more than you deserve it."

"But Phil's not qualified," Billy said.

"He's qualified, Billy."

"Okay, then I guess you gotta give the job to Phil. I give you my consent."

"Thanks, Billy, for your consent."

"You're welcome. I'll probably need to walk him through what I do. It can get pretty complicated."

"We'll handle it, Billy."

"Ok, that's fine. Tell Phil that I give him my consent."

"Ok, Billy."

"I guess I'll go back to my desk now."

THE ESCAPIST

"Ok, Billy."

On the third and last day of work, Billy left before noon, and when he got home, he packed up the Nissan systematically, first with two bags of his clothes, then his folding chair, then his sleeping bag, a pillow, waterproof hiking boots, a few books of fiction that he had snagged from the free books shelf at Cobin-Haskett, a deck of cards, his passport, and then his cooler of paraphernalia and illicits which he had kept on the floor of the closet of his bedroom. Last to be packed was his array of back-to-front sticky notes re-adhered to one another and sorted out in piles and finally wrapped with rubber bands. The first two sticky notes at the top of the pile listed his current stock levels:

> Cannabis: slightly less than 1 lb
> MDMA: 80mgs, 48 tablets
> Diazepam: 2mgs, 53 tablets
> Psilocybin: approx. 1/2 lb
> mushroom caps/stems
> Psilocin analogue: 6 tablets,
> 4-sub tryptamine
> Alprazolam: Xanax, 0.5mgs,
> 96 count

> Oxycontin: 10mgs, 75 tablets
> Percocet: 5mgs, 26 tablets
> Dexedrine: 10mgs, 17 tablets
> Adderall: 25mgs,
> time-release capsules, 64 tablets
> Clonazepam: 0.5mgs, 42 tablets
> Cocaine: 2 eightballs, approx.
> 6 grams

He left his mattress and broken dresser along with some other stuff on the curb. Billy picked up Speedy, his pet turtle, and played with him for a little while. He lay down on the barren floor and let Speedy crawl across his chest. He watched as a few mucus bubbles popped out of Speedy's nostrils. He put him back in his small tank, put the container of turtle feed in the tank as well, picked up the tank and walked over to his neighbor's apartment. He put the tank down at the doorstep, rang the doorbell and then ran away as fast as he could. Stuck to the side of the tank was a sticky note that read:

> Hello neighbor,
> I'm leaving the city now. I hope you can give Speedy the turtle a good home. I hope you can give him love because I unfortunately was not the best daddy and am now leaving him in your expert care. Good luck. And thanks. And sorry. I hope you will love him and I'm sure that in time he will grow to love you too.

There was minimal traffic on the George Washington Bridge, the Palisades Parkway was clear and green, the sky a deep blue with a few lush clouds overhead. An auspicious start.

After five and a half hours driving northwest, he reached Brevard Farm. It consisted of one large farmhouse where Felix resided along with Miss Priss and Frank, his two feline friends, and there were four small barns, one with a large greenhouse, and a silo farther down on the property. In addition to the corn and corn grain, floriculture, and in-season fruits and vegetables, the barns also contained Felix's real pride and joy: he was a collector of antiques and other unique items, which were scattered about the barns and the farmhouse. In the farmhouse he saw vintage furniture, dusty books from generations past, odd paintings and sculptures, old cash registers, rusted out advertising signs, hundreds of old bobble-heads, and an oversized head of a buffalo, which must have weighed fifty pounds. Felix also stored in one of the barns almost a dozen old motorcycles, many with missing parts and flat tires.

After Felix had given him a tour, Billy wandered around on his own to get a better feel for his surroundings, and he found seemingly endless rows of cornstalks which eventually opened into roaming fields with spruce and oak trees. Between the barns he saw thousands of plants and flowers in various gardens, and many hundreds more all encapsulated in their own utopias of marble and plaster pots. Eight skittish peacocks lived on the property, and Felix told him that one of the females had laid an egg in the boxed-in veranda of one of the barns. Felix had waited and watched as the mother peacock nurtured her egg until it was ripe for hatching, but a weasel snuck in one morning and ate the unborn peachick for breakfast. Felix told him he might sometimes see an occasional wolf or coyote, probably some weary deer, and he would most likely encounter his two outdoor homeless cats, Beauregard and Mustafa, who had braved it through the cold winter.

Billy started working around the property the following morning. He did some landscaping—he preferred the term landscaping over gardening to fortify his sense of manliness; in fact, one of the other groundskeepers whom he was shadowing on that first day felt the same way and called it manscaping. Billy did a lot of heavy lifting, shuffling items around from place to place, mostly bulky bags of corn grain, lawn mowing, hedge trimming, weeding, spraying. Felix promised that soon after Billy got his feet wet, he would have Joe, his head groundskeeper, give him a full tutorial on using the combine harvester, what he considered the single most important piece of equipment on the farm. It was a large clunker of a machine, and although Billy really did not care one way or another if he got to use it, Felix acted as though he owned the Holy Grail, and Billy should be honored.

Felix bought most of his meals, cooked hearty 5AM breakfasts, when he told his most recent Williamson stories. Felix recently had learned how to use EBay and had gone from novice to top buyer within a few months. He discussed some of his more recent purchases with Billy, notably a 1966 gold base bobblehead of Willie Mays which he predicted was worth thousands more than what he was buying it for. He also paid a fortune for an old tin Fleetwood Tires sign.

There was a science to Felix's unorthodox arrangement of vases and statues and mirrors and toys and postcards and other relics. A cluttered yet distinguished feel of Americana populated the farm. But this caused functional problems: he couldn't use any of the tables or desks in the farmhouse. He could only take baths and not showers because he had a large collection of soaps and old apothecary bottles stacked on top of each other in the shower stall. He could sleep only on one side of his bed because the other side had stacks of newspapers, books, journals, notebooks, sketchpads, as if they were the replacement for the body of a loved one. As Billy looked down upon the bed, he saw that the front page of the newspaper on the top of the stack was about the growing Occupy Wall Street movement, not just in New York City, but across the country.

After a few weeks of this, Billy started to feel like this was a life for someone much older. He was seventeen years younger than Felix's next youngest groundskeeper. Not enough privacy for his liking. Felix or one of his workers always seemed to be creeping around the corner. And though it was a big old farm on seventy acres, Billy could never find adequate space to himself to do what he wanted to do, which was nothing at all except trip out and melt away to constantly evolving stimuli. Thoughts of fleeing, again, were becoming more frequent.

Billy came to see the farm as an extension of Felix himself. He found it to be just as cluttered and amuck as Felix's mind. Felix jumped from one project to the next, always preoccupied with new missions. There were so many missed opportunities in Felix's own life, Billy learned, so many wishes left unfulfilled, so many dreams never fully realized, and the grounds were a representation of that. Two of the barns farther down on the property had water-damaged floors, but the important collections were always carefully maintained. Felix had other collections of various old items that sat piled in corners all over each of the barns and at the farmhouse, and maintenance of these items was almost nonexistent. They were just collecting dust and perpetually in wait for their time to be tinkered with again because of a renewed dedication from Felix, but it usually never came. He was like Billy in that sense, dedicated to the next thing. Many of Felix's collections were the products of really great ideas only partially realized, left for dead.

This new way of life here at the farm soon translated into a chaotic meaningless existence, for he tried to picture himself in it, was happy enough for those few weeks, but there would still be the cold sweats and tremors at night. Billy, at one point, as he was getting ready for bed, seemingly out of nowhere, fell into a rage, punched at the air and then fell upon his bed and screamed into his pillow. It scared him because it reminded him of his father, and then it made him angry again, and he screamed some more into the pillow. That night Billy decided to leave.

The next day, in the late afternoon, Billy packed the Nissan with his belongings in a mad rush, and when he went into the farmhouse for the last of his things, some clothes, his sleeping bag, and Bubba, he saw Felix staring inquisitively.

"Where you off to so soon?" he asked him. "You only just got here!"

Billy didn't answer for a moment. He just looked down at the pile of stuff in his hands. He looked down at Bubba. "I need to go find my dad," was his answer. Why this came out of his mouth, he was unsure. He felt he had been able to put his life with Alan behind him—he didn't need to open that book again. He was sweating, and Felix stared into his dilated pupils. He lifted up Billy's eyelids and looked into his puffy eyes.

"I have a problem," Billy said to him next, bashfully, turning away. "I have a very bad problem."

"You know, we can get you some help, son. I know some good people up here that you can talk to."

"I don't need help. People have already tried to help. It just makes it worse. I just have to go. Thank you for everything." He turned to walk away.

"Will you be coming back?"

"I don't think so."

"Did you talk to Nicole about this?"

"No, I haven't talked to her."

"Don't you think she'll be upset about your decision?"

"No, I don't, well, she, well, maybe. Well, yea."

"I think so."

"I'm sorry, but I need to go. I made a mistake."

"I don't know if I can let you drive like this."

"Well, I don't know if you'll be able to stop me."

"I can call the cops—how about that?"

"That's not going to do you any good. These are prescription medications. I'm on very serious prescription medications. You don't know shit about me."

"Last time I checked, you can still get a DUI for that."

"I'm fine. I am perfectly fine. Please just let me go."

"You don't seem fine to me, my boy. Please, just take a seat. Let me get you something to drink. Just sit."

He sat Billy down on the wooden bench by the kitchen, set the last of Billy's things on the splintered floor, went into the kitchen to grab some water, and Billy jumped up and ran for the door. He leaped down the front stairs and into his car, started the ignition, and sped quickly for about twenty feet then stopped. He hit his head on the steering wheel a few times and then turned the car off. He slowly walked back over to the house. Felix was standing in the doorway.

"I'm sorry," Billy said coyly. "I forgot my…Look. I'm just…I'm sorry to be like this. I just have a—"

"—a problem, I know."

"Well this is going to fuck everything up with Nicole now, isn't it? You're going to tell her about this, aren't you. Yea, you are. Please, just, please let me be the one to talk to her first."

"Does she know about the prescriptions? About the drugs?"

"No. She doesn't want to know about this stuff. No one wants to know about this stuff."

"Billy, I'm not going to call the damn police. If you

want to leave, just drive the hell on outta here, and I ain't gonna stop you. You're a good kid. You were a good worker for me. I won't talk to Nicole about this. If she calls, I'll just tell her that you left and that she should speak to you directly. You know why I'm doing this?"

"No."

"Because I can understand what you're going through. You remind me of me, a little bit, Billy."

"I do?" Billy's eyes opened widely, hopefully.

"Well, maybe not in some ways. But in other ways, sure. Let me give you some advice that someone once tried to give me, something that would have helped me before I got too deep in all this," he waved his arms in a circle pointing at everything and nothing. "You gotta let it all go. You gotta be able to forgive. And you have to find it in yourself. It's in here," he said pointing to his own heart.

"Cheesy shit," Billy said under his breath.

"It's right in there," Felix said more loudly now pointing at Billy's heart, doing so with more urgency. "I don't know if someone hurt you. Or why. Why anyone would've wanted to hurt you. But I think someone did hurt you, and you can't keep it buried. Someone hurt me too. If you keep it buried like I did for a long time, then you'll just keep burying everything else until there's nothing else left. Until there's nowhere else to dig. Your whole world will end up underground. And that's where you'll end up. Underground."

"No one hurt me." Billy went into the house, picked up the last of his things on the floor and went back past Felix and put them in the trunk.

Felix followed him to the car. "Do something for me, Billy," Felix said abruptly and turned him around by his shoulder. "I don't know if you've ever tried this. But write it down—just write it all down. It works for me anyway. It helps. A sentence, a paragraph, a page, anything you want to write about. Anything at all. Just write it down. Nobody needs to see it. And nobody gets to read it. You may just find some hidden pathways you never knew existed, some pathways that may help you."

Billy listened with his head to the ground, then got into his car. A peacock strutted past them.

"Billy, you promise?"

"Yea, yea, I promise."

"Shake on it."

Billy reached his hand out through the car window and they held hands for a moment.

"Thank you, Billy. Please come back whenever you'd like." It was then when Felix handed him the journal. It was a small black college-ruled notebook with a poly cover. The glue in the binding still had a salubrious scent as though it had just been manufactured.

Billy drove to the interstate and kept on driving. "Your heart is black," he said to his reflection in the rearview mirror. *Your heart is black. Black as night, dead and gone.*

7

Upon his arrival in Savannah, Billy felt the strangeness of being a newcomer to an old city, a city he knew nothing about. His hostel in Savannah was old but had fresh young beautiful faces. It was the second floor of an old church building. It was like a co-op, and people could do chores in order to pay less in rent. It seemed reasonable enough. The young fresh face that greeted Billy when he walked in was the one who doled out the responsibilities. Billy's duty was to clean the bathrooms. He was shown his room. All the beds in the room were empty except one which had a fellow barricaded by his bike making it hard to see him. He had a big travel backpack leaning up against the bed. A racing suit was on a hanger from the top bunk.

"You do your chores every other day before noon. So you would start doing your chores tomorrow morning."

She showed Billy where the cleaning supplies were in the bathroom.

"You'll mop down these floors and the shower stalls, scrub the toilets and toilet seats, clean the mirrors."

Billy nodded his head in agreement. *Anything to save a buck.*

"Did somebody by the name of Alan Chute stay here like three weeks ago?"

"Not that I know of. Sorry."

The next day he walked around the old city. It was hot—over ninety degrees. Billy tried to imagine that he was his father, tried to put himself in his shoes. Everyone he saw was his father. Every face was his. Every face wasn't. He learned of River Street through a talk he had with a young guy on a bicycle with a grayish, probably previously white shirt at Forsyth Park: "It's a street downtown on the water where you can walk around with an open container. You can just go from one bar to the next without having to put down your drink. You can chill at the benches at the water, just get wasted. I'm heading over there if you want to come."

That sounds like a place Dad would be. Why not.

They walked through the park squares, passed some of the enchanted cotton warehouses where slaves had worked with broken backs for their masters. During their walk the guy asked Billy what his story was. He told him that he was a tourist, here to take in the city.

"I got some smoky treats, too, if you're interested," his hippy companion said.

"How much?"

"How much you want?"

"What can a hundo get me."

"A quarter of kind, my good man."

"Where you want to do this?" Billy asked. Billy's weed stash was running low, and he knew he needed to replenish it. It still helped him from thinking about himself, but it would instead, he'd later find out, just welcome the thoughts back.

River Street ran parallel to the water and was lined with bars and restaurants, tattoo parlors, gift shops, tourist traps. There was a beautiful view of the distant ships and vanishing horizon. The two of them stopped into a smoothie bar where all that was being sold were liquor-instilled chilled concoctions. The choices: Strawberry, Pina Colada, Monkey Shine, Shock Treatment, Green Apple, Call-A-Cab, Attitude Improvement, Sex on the Beach, Mojitorojo, Fruit Punch-In-The-Face, Angry Sailor. Billy showed the bartender his ID, still with that callow glee of being able to show he was finally of legal drinking age. Billy elected for Angry Sailor, and followed the young hippy to the bathroom to do the transaction.

The young hippy pulled his dick out to pee.

"Damn, man."

"You interested in anything else?"

"Fuck you," Billy said after glancing at his cock.

"Nah man, not that. I got some mushies, too. Acid? Some tranqs, bennies…?"

"You got any Codeine? Demerol?"

"Nah, but I got some Vike."

Billy left the bathroom, restocked, and walked around the area, looking for a familiar face. He eventually came to a bench overlooking the ocean and decided it was a good place to stop, and as dusk was emerging around him, he *prayed* like how Uncle George did it. He whispered and repeated, "Please God, please."

Finding one person in a big city is close to impossible, he thought. It's even harder to find traces of that person if he had already moved on to his next destination. Billy probably would have been in Savannah for weeks searching for remnants of a ghost, if it weren't for Nicole. His zen state of disquietude sitting there on the bench overlooking the ocean was quickly interrupted when his cell phone buzzed in his pocket.

"What the hell are you doing in Savannah?" she asked when he told her where he was.

"Just stopping by to see my father. Say hi."

"I didn't know your father lived in Savannah."

"Yea, well, he does."

"How long you planning on staying?"

"I don't know yet, I haven't decided."

"Well, I'm working a flight on Thursday night to Miami. And I got the weekend off. You ever been to

Miami before? You should come meet me. I haven't seen you since New York. And you still haven't even told me why you left. When I asked Felix about it, he got quiet and weird. But you can explain later, ok? I just want to see you."

"I don't know. I just got here. I haven't even done that much around the city yet."

"What's wrong with you? Don't you want to see me? You'll have the next few days to do stuff. Hang with your dad a bit, and then come hang out with me for the weekend, and then you can go back to Savannah next week, or wherever else you're going. It'll be fun. I promise. It's, what, like an eight-hour drive from Savannah? Eight hours aren't bad."

"Nah, I can't. I really can't. I have to stick to the plan. I got a plan, you know?"

"Free hotel room, Billy. Right on the beach. Think about it."

An hour passed and she called him back. "Ok, now you definitely have to come to Miami. You don't have a choice now."

"What are you talking about?"

"You come meet me in Miami and then we're going to go on an adventure for the weekend. You're not going to believe this. I was able to get tickets through work for a weekend cruise from Miami to the Bahamas! And then back again! We'll be back in Miami by Monday morning. Plus, my friends Macy and Victor want to come along too. I got four passes so we'll have a little couple's getaway. You remember me telling you about Macy and Victor right? They're awesome. You're gonna love them. It'll be fun, a perfect little escape."

Maybe Peter was right. "Alright already! Alright! I'll come. It'll be fun. It'll be fun..."

He drank many more alcohol-infused smoothies and was wasted by 10PM. Many of the night owls on the strip were just getting started. He didn't remember how he made it back to the hostel, but he woke on the bottom of the bunk bed, even though he was assigned the top one.

After you had been at Brevard Farm in Williamson for something like a week, Nicole was home for the weekend and wanted to pay you and her uncle Felix a surprise visit. She drove over to the property on Saturday evening, and you had already finished your work for the day. The sun had not quite set, and you, not knowing that she was coming, had taken a walk around the farm, over to the open expanse past the cornfields. You smoked a few pinners on your walk, some tobacco and cannabis salads, and you had taken a few of your other dosages a few hours earlier. When you got back to the house, she was there, sitting with Felix at the dining table with a cup of tea.

--There he is!
--Wow! Nicole! Wow! You're here!"

--I'm here!

She got up, walked over to you, hugged you. Kissing didn't feel quite natural yet, and you didn't know whether it was appropriate to do so with Felix watching. Good that you used eye drops and put in some gum before walking into the house.

--Pull up a chair, Felix said. Tell us how everything's going.

--Everything's great so far. Felix is great. This place is amazing...I didn't know you were going to be here.

--One of my flights got rerouted. I don't fly back out until Tuesday morning. It was a terrible ride though. So much turbulence and this one guy wouldn't stop throwing up.

--Nicole was telling me how you guys first met, Felix said, suddenly changing the subject.

--She did? You clammed up.

--Yup, she told me all about it.

--Oh, well, what did she tell you?

--I told him the truth, Nicole said.

--The truth, Felix repeated.

--So anyway, Nicole continued, the pilot was clearly not feeling well either, and the whole time this kid in the back kept crying something awful and had this bad barking cough.

Felix's comment had to be in reference to something they had been discussing before you came in. They may have just had that kind of open relationship where she could tell him about her sexual escapades, that she had sex with you the first night she met you.

--People think that we automatically like kids in our line of work. Such a load of shit. I hate kids. Why do you think I took

a job that sends me away for most of the year? And then two days ago, outside of Miami, I was visiting Macy. So she and I went out with her husband, Victor, and some of their other friends. We got so shitfaced.

--Speaking of, drink? Felix asked.

--Sure.

--Beer?

--Sure.

Nicole went upstairs to change a few minutes later, and after she sat back down at the table, she was applying a skin mask to her face.

You picked up the tin can and read the label. It consisted of mud and folic acid, the mud being a sacred substance from some body of water containing curative ingredients that would heal any strange manifestation on the face. No wonder her skin gets so silky, you thought. She has to rely on her face for her livelihood. The face has to be presentable, unblemished.

--What? she said, seeing you staring as she was smearing on her blackface.

--Nothing.

But there was something. You were wondering in that moment what the fuck you were doing there, with this woman, with her uncle, at some farm in the middle of nowhere. Desperation. Loneliness.

Nicole was particularly horny that evening. Then, she was gone. And you weren't that far behind her.

Billy remembered his chores. He polished the floors of the bathroom, wiped down the sink, the mirror, the shower stalls, then made calls to other local hostels to see if they had any record of his father. No luck. He walked to the 120-bed shelter of the Salvation Army of Savannah. Each bed was occupied. None of them had his father, and they were not permitted to provide names of those that had stayed there in the past. Nor did he have any success with Grace House of UMI, Inner City Night Shelter, Park Place Outreach, J.C. Lewis Health Center, Interfaith Hospitality Network, the Habersham House, Potters of UMI, the Men's Residential, the Housing Authority of Savannah, the Savannah Area Behavioral Health Collaborative, all dead ends.

Days of searching had passed, and he had not even been able to unearth one small lead. It was a beautiful city, but no trace of Alan. Billy got back in the Nissan and drove down the coast toward Miami. Every few hours he would stop to fill up his tank, his car's and his own—gas for the Nissan, and for him, the other kinds of gas, what he had at his disposal in the cooler. It helped sustain the vision of whom he called his girlfriend as his shining bastion of hope, and when it started to dim, he knew it was time to fill up again. There was a new budding approach to filling up his tank as well, and it was growing on him: putting pen to paper. By now he had filled twenty-six pages of the notebook Felix had given him. He had found his father only in there.

8

Billy awoke with his head spinning, hurting, lost in a hotel room bed and suddenly pushed out of it, and Nicole's muffled voice was yelling something at him. He rubbed his eyes—"hurry the fuck up!" she was roaring. It was Friday morning.

Billy tossed some clothes and belongings for the trip into his backpack, threw in his bag of weed, quickly counted out pills and shuffled some into different bottles and then tossed them in too, just the bare essentials. He locked everything else in the trunk of the car. Their taxi to the port of Miami was twenty-five minutes late. Victor had run off to find an ATM machine. They were all incredibly hung over from the previous night's festivities. They all drank liquor the night before, and Billy was able to sneak in his narcotics on the side. Victor and Macy could party hard, and they all lost their minds on the dance floor of a nearby Miami nightclub. Billy had never really liked to dance and didn't want to, but before he knew it, he was bobbing up and down like a pogo stick to the music, with his eyes closed, smiling, raging, letting it all go for the night. He loved being able to let it all go.

Once Victor returned, they were waiting for him inside the taxi, and he jumped in. They were supposed to board the cruise in only a few minutes. Victor called the port and told them that the four of them were on their way. The woman on the phone said that they would be able to hold the vessel for another ten minutes but after that, if they weren't on board, the boat would leave without them.

Victor gave the taxi driver an extra twenty-dollar bill and told him to floor it. When they pulled up to the port, they grabbed their bags and ran as fast as they could through the turnstiles to get to the loading dock. Billy hadn't even considered the fact that security would be there waiting for them. They put their bags on the conveyor belt to be screened then walked through the metal detectors. Billy was the last one to go through. He didn't trigger any alarms, but there was a questionable item in his backpack. The guard thought a screwdriver was in his bag when in actuality it was his electric toothbrush. He asked Billy's permission to search the bag. Billy didn't realize how meticulous the guard would be. After not discovering a screwdriver or anything of the sort, the guard continued to search through the smaller zippered pockets of the backpack and it was then when he discovered the meds. Then the pot.

"What's this?" the guard asked Billy, holding up the bag of greenery.

"It's marijuana."

The guard got on his walky-talky and called for assistance. Almost instantly, Billy was surrounded by fifteen homeland security officers while the deputy of the cruise was staring coldly in his direction. Another delay for the cruise ship. Nicole was also staring, dumbfounded. He pleaded with some of the officers to look the other way before the handcuffs were locked around his wrists. Nicole stayed behind, as he would need someone to bail him out. So Macy and Victor set sail without them. Billy was hauled off to Miami-Dade County lockdown.

The back of the cop car was cramped and uncomfortable. There was no legroom and Billy was sitting against his cuffed hands. He didn't speak unless spoken to. The driver had Billy's passport but asked him for all of his personal information anyway. He gave it willingly. When they arrived at the jail, they drove through an automated electric gate topped with barbed wire. Billy entered a secure area where he was processed. They took his fingerprints and his mug shot. He was stripped out of all his clothes for a full cavity search.

"Stick out your tongue. Good. Lift your arms. Good. Spread your legs. Good. Turn around. Touch your toes. Good."

Billy had remnants of a hemorrhoid and was self-conscious about the guard seeing it. His dick was practically inside his body.

Billy cupped what was left of his privates with one hand and stood with his head down. The guard patted his clothes and then tossed them back at Billy. There were other men getting their full-cavity searches in the room. Dressed now, Billy was taken to a payphone and was informed that he had three minutes to make a call. Unfortunately, the only phone numbers he knew were cell phones and the payphone couldn't make a collect call to a cellular. Billy could have called Cynthia but still didn't want to speak to her, and he knew Uncle George and Aunt Tracy's home phone number, but he was not about to tell them. Billy waited patiently at the phone dock until he received further instruction. There was another newly-detained prisoner at the phone dock, and he said to Billy: "You got no one to call?"

"No one to call."

"Can't you call your parents?"

"My parents are dead."

A line of inmates careened past him. Billy was blown a kiss by one of them. He was taken to a holding cell about the size of his old living room. There were approximately a dozen or so other offenders in the cell with him.

There was no bench space so he took a seat on the floor. There was a single toilet in the cell; it was backed up with a brown liquid and ready to overflow onto the floor upon which he was sitting. *You're going to have to hold it.* He saw some cockroaches crawling around the cell, some hiding in cracks in the walls while others roamed unreservedly in and out of the cell and elsewhere. Billy didn't want to look at any of his cellmates. He had never been thrown into a real jail cell before, and he didn't know what to expect. Mission Mountain was prison, but it was nothing like the real thing. His better judgment told him not to say anything to anyone and never make eye contact. He heard multiple languages. A lot of broken English. He pulled his t-shirt over his head. He counted to 1,000.

"Line up!" someone yelled from outside the cell. Billy warily pulled his shirt down off of his face. More people had been put in the cell. It was getting crowded. A guard was standing outside with a box of sandwiches wrapped in Saran Wrap. They looked to Billy like balls of shit. The cellmates lined up and waited to receive their sandwiches.

"You gonna eat your sandwich?" asked a skinny boy who had been sleeping when Billy first entered the cell.

Billy shook his head.

"Can I have yours then?"

Billy nodded his head.

"Get in line then!" he shrieked.

Billy jumped to his feet and did as the boy wished. When the guard handed Billy the balled sandwich, his fingernail scratched the back of Billy's hand. Billy pulled his hand back and accidentally squished the sandwich with his fingers. He handed it to the boy and apologized. The boy grabbed it, unwrapped it quickly, and shoved the entire thing into his mouth. Billy's spot on the floor was now occupied and sitting space was in short supply. Billy found some available floor space in the center of the cell. All the wall space was occupied. Billy put his shirt back over his head and leaned forward. He counted to 1,000.

A female guard would pop her head in every twenty minutes or so and yell that such and such made bail. Such and such was then ushered out of the cell. Billy couldn't understand why his name hadn't been called yet. *It was just weed. Just some prescription pills. You should have been the first one out of here.*

With his shirt still over his head, he suddenly felt a sharp blow to his face. He was pretty sure it was a foot. He felt he deserved it. He toppled over onto a cellmate. He pushed Billy off of him, and Billy toppled onto another body. Billy's shirt was still over his head and practically off of his body at this point, so he couldn't see what was going on. It was just dark and painful. The second person that he landed on had removed the shirt off of Billy's head. The bright fluorescent lights from above stung Billy's eyes, and it took him a few seconds to adjust to it. Billy's head was lying in his lap. There was a larger crowd of people in the cell now. Many of them were staring right at him. He had a bloody lip and was shirtless. He sat up and saw he had wet himself. His nose felt cracked and his gums were sore. He had no idea who kicked him, and he didn't want to know. He just wanted to get the fuck out of that holding cell. He slid his body back to the wall, and he kept pushing his body into it with his feet, like if he could just push hard enough he could dissolve through it and disappear.

✕ ✕ ✕

Billy's thoughts would roam to random experiences he and his father shared, memories he hadn't thought about in years, and soon they came flooding in. They destroyed any semblance of peace he was trying to maintain. He wondered what Nicole was going through while he was in here.

Billy could see the sun going down through the miniature-caged window in the back of the cell. His name still had not been called. Billy had been arrested in the early morning, and the sun would set around 8PM, so he assumed at least eight hours had passed at this point.

Billy thought about Macy and Victor, kicking back on the deck of the vessel, sipping mojitos, watching the sunset, clinking their glasses together and drinking to freedom. *Why. Are you still in this shitbox.*

The dynamics of the holding cell changed after the sun went down. The werewolves emerged. Not only did the number of people triple, but Billy was no longer the only white boy. Time just continued to lag. "Jail sucks," one of the patrons continued to repeat to himself while rapidly shaking his leg, a nervous tick. "Jail sucks, God, jail sucks." The more people that entered the holding cell, the more chaotic things became. It was beginning to feel like a New York City subway during rush hour, except with criminals—scary-looking criminals. Fights were breaking out and guards would enter the cell every twenty minutes or so to remove violent offenders they caught in the act.

From one of the corners of the cell, Billy heard someone yell, "Hey you! You! YOU!" Billy *prayed* that he was shouting to someone else in the cell. And if Billy was the one that he was shouting at, Billy *prayed* that he wanted his attention for a simple reason, not for anything harmful, aggravated, or sexual.

Billy shouldn't have even looked. If he hadn't looked in his direction then the man might have given up and moved on to someone else. But he looked. The man had a bald head, big eyes, a few gold teeth. When he knew Billy was listening, he continued: "Come over here—let me talk to you for a minute." Billy shook his head and kept his eyes to the ground. "Don't ignore me—you come over here." Billy shook his head again. He kept shaking his head. The man stood up. *Oh fuck*. He weaved through the crowd toward him. *Fuck, fuck, FUCK*. Billy thought about shitting his pants. It had worked as a deterrent in the past. He should have. Maybe the man would have left him alone. But he didn't.

"Stand up."

"I think I would rather sit."

"Stand the fuck up!"

Billy slowly stood up but kept his head down. The man put his hand under Billy's chin and raised his head so he could look Billy in the face.

"You look all fucked up!" the man said smiling. "Your face is all puffy." The man rubbed his fingers down Billy's face. "Who did this to you?"

"I don't know."

"Just tell me who did this to you."

"I don't know."

"You don't know who did this to you?"

"I don't—"

"*I* did this to you."

Billy dropped his head back down to the ground.

"You want to hit me back?"

Billy shook his head in silence.

"Hit me back."

Billy continued shaking his head.

THE ESCAPIST

"You better hit me back. Didn't you hear me, I'm the one that kicked you! Hit me back! Get some!"

Billy *prayed* for the female guard to walk into the cell and call his name. He envisioned her walking in right when he was about to get violated; he envisioned his name getting called and escaping to freedom, stepping outside of the cell, and waving goodbye, good riddance, go fuck yourself; he envisioned the tormenter locking his lips, lowering his eyebrows and pumping his fist in anger, and our hero smiling ear to ear and blowing the man a kiss goodbye.

× × ×

It took twenty-two hours for Billy to be released from Miami-Dade lockdown. The Florida penal system was set up so that a drug offense like Billy's could potentially earn him the brunt force of the law. Luckily, the system was so backed up with offenders more serious than himself that he could also end up not serving time in prison at all. He found out after leaving Miami-Dade lockdown that apparently, the state of Florida had some of the harshest marijuana and drug laws in the country. Besides the pot, the majority of his pills were prescription meds with his name on the labels; however, some of the bottles had some other narcotics mixed in. He was partially relieved that he didn't have *more* drugs on him. Still, he was looking at Class B felonies. Billy knew he should have been smarter. He knew he should've dosed right after waking up to not make such a stupid mistake. He considered and reconsidered his course of action that morning. He also realized that it was just a matter of time until something like this happened.

It was a male guard that finally entered the cell to release him from custody. The female guard's shift must have ended. He called his name. Billy was half-delusional when he announced it. He had to announce it again and then a third time for Billy to recognize that it was his name the guard was calling. Billy made bail. He stood up out of a cramped ball position and was finally escorted to freedom.

A droning buzz sounded which unlocked the front gate, and he walked out of it with two other inmates that were being released at the same time. It was the early morning when he walked out. The sky was freshly painted with sunlight, and he had hardly slept. One of the other inmates jumped in celebration when he was released. The inmate took off his shirt, and his body was tatted up with black ink graffiti careening down his neck to his lower back, chest and arms. He swung his shirt around above his head. There was a car parked on the street blasting music with an earth-shattering bass-drum shaking the foundations of all that was good in Billy's world. The guy ran over to the car, lifted open the trunk where a change of clothes was waiting for him. He undressed right there on the street, put on the fresh clothes, hopped in, and they sped off.

There was a little waiting area on the outside of the prison with a few picnic benches, but no Nicole. Billy wondered how long she had actually waited before giving up. He wondered if she had gotten any sleep. He felt like he was waking up from a very bad dream, or coming down from a bad acid trip.

Nicole had all of his belongings including his cell phone, so he had no way to get in touch with her. She had his wallet with all of his cash and credit cards. He had the clothes on his back and his passport, which was returned after. He sat outside, wondering if Nicole would show up.

A few people were sitting beside him. There was trash everywhere. Billy's body was aching, his face still in pain. He stretched out on the bench, closed his eyes and was dozing in minutes.

Suddenly, he was shaken awake. He sat up, smiled at her. Nicole had big bags under her eyes, and her hair was up in a tight ponytail. She wasn't wearing any make-up. It was the first time he ever saw her in public without it.

"You don't know what I've been through over the last twenty-four hours," she said.

"I'm so sorry, Nicole."

"Oh my God. Look at your face." Her throat made a clicking noise. "What did they do to you in there."

"I'd rather not talk about it right now. I just want to get the fuck away from this place."

"I have a hotel room booked through the weekend." She turned and walked away without looking back. Billy followed.

At the hotel, Billy undressed and showered. The scorching hot water felt good. Billy stood under it for a while, lost in a daze. He dried off and crawled under the covers. They ordered food and watched TV. He ate in bed, eventually fell asleep, and he slept a deep dark empty sleep. He was impenetrable from any dreams or nightmares or any subconscious thoughts. He was dead weight, good and gone. He slept through the remainder of the early evening into the night and woke to the rising of the sun. Nicole was still fast asleep. Under the desk in the hotel room was his bag, and he reached inside for his journal.

9

It's funny how the brain can turn memories into nothing. How your brain knows what's best, and it chooses memories and hides others. But then something happens, something can force a bad memory back into existence. What's it like? It's like someone taking your head and turning it on its side, bashing on it until the memory melts out of your ear cavity into their hand for them to grab and then splash over your eye sockets. Without warning. And it will disturb, disturb, conquer any of the happiness that you think you've finally found for yourself.

It's funny how the brain can lose its ability to hold on to the good memories. Sometimes you're forced to focus on things that happened so long ago because everything else just turns into sewage. It's funny how sometimes the most beautiful memories are lost forever and you're stuck with the ones that remind you of how awful people can be, how brutal and barbaric people can be, how disturbed and grisly people can be. How you are nothing but the same.

Remember when Dad would place you in front of the TV?

THE ESCAPIST

You were too old for Sesame Street, but he didn't care. It was actually nice to watch. It was peaceful. It had a certain comfort, like Xanax for the first time. Yea, so this time when Dad sat you down in front of the TV, Peter was outside playing in the mud. Dad made you a tuna fish sandwich. He made one for himself as well. He joined you in the living room, and the two of you sat and watched the television program, quietly. Soberly. But he was watching you more than actually watching the TV screen, wasn't he? Staring at you. He was thinking about killing you, wasn't he? It's that look he would get. This was maybe the first time you saw it, with him sitting there chewing down that tuna fish sandwich. The moment when you first felt like he wanted to rip your fucking heart out. End your life for ending hers. End your life to end his own. How many times was it that he had tried?

And he would sometimes say her name, wouldn't he? Yes, in the beginning, he did. Yes, he would say that this was for her. Yes, for you both to feel her again. Yes, he would say. Yes. And sometimes it did kinda feel like she was there.

Nicole eventually woke and saw him sitting up in bed next to her with his journal in his lap. She didn't ask about it, didn't seem to care, showered, and then ordered more room service. Billy ate his scrambled eggs, bacon, and buttered toast still under the covers. The swelling on his face went down a little, but his body continued to ache.

"Nicole, I still don't want to talk about it. All I want to say is that I'm sorry. I'm sorry you weren't able to take the cruise this weekend. I'm sorry you had to bail me out of jail. I'll pay you back. How much was it anyway?"

"Seventeen hundred bucks. But you aren't going to have to pay me back, the state will take care of that. What you need to worry about is finding a lawyer. You're gonna have to go to court for this, you know."

"How much do lawyers cost?"

"Lawyers are fucking expensive. Really fucking expensive. When Macy got a DWI last year, she ended up losing over six grand by the time everything was settled out of court. I hate to be the one to break this to you, but the money you saved up for this little getaway of yours, you're going to need it for this now. Consider this your last stop."

"No. That's not the way it works. Money isn't going to get in the way. Money's never gotten in the way. I can make it work. That's what credit cards are for right?"

"Christ, Billy. That's the stupidest thing I've ever heard. Save your money, as much as you can, and get a lawyer. If you don't get a lawyer, then you're going to be fucked by the time your court date rolls around. You'll end up having to go back to jail. You want that? A lawyer might be able to make this whole thing go away."

Fuck. Fuck. Fuck. Billy sat up in bed. He rocked back and forth. He put his hands on top of his head and tried yanking the hair out of his skull. "I need to keep going.

I can't just quit. Not this time. I need to find him."

"Find who?"

"There's just someone I'm looking for. I haven't been able to find him yet."

"Listen to me, Billy. Forget about this little road trip you're taking. You need to worry about your future. Your career. You think people are going to want to hire a drug addict?"

"I'm not a fucking drug addict," he said softly. "It was just a little bit of pot."

"More than a little bit. Plus that prescription shit. What do you need all those pills for?"

"I—I have some medical stuff going on."

"Medical, my ass. No one needs all those pills. What kind of doctor prescribes all that shit to one person?"

"Doctor*s*."

"Who *are* you, Billy?"

"I'm Billy Chute. Just a normal guy. I'm a regular fucking guy. I mean, this could have happened to anybody."

"Yea, anybody who is stupid enough to try to sneak drugs through customs."

"Fuck you."

"No, fuck you, Billy. You don't know what you put me through, you fucking asshole." Waterworks. "I had to sit outside of a piece of shit prison and let low life degenerate assholes rub up on me and call me names. Names that I am not about to repeat. I was sitting there all alone, in my skimpy fucking sundress waiting for my asshole baby boyfriend to be released."

"Listen, I'm sorry. How many times do you need me to say it. I'm sorry. I'm so fucking sorry."

"How long have you been smoking dope?"

"I don't know. A while."

"What's a while?"

"I don't know. A while."

"I can't go out with a drug addict."

"Nicole. I'm not a fucking drug addict. Get your head out of the gutter. I'm not fucking freebasing. I'm not sticking fucking needles into my arms." *Anymore.* "Those fucking cancer sticks you smoke are a hundred times worse than smoking weed. Soon pot is going to be perfectly legal and cigarettes are going to be what people are going to jail for."

"I don't want to have a debate. But you have to make me a promise."

"What's that."

"You're never gonna smoke that stuff ever again. And you're never gonna do anymore of that other shit either."

"I'll stop smoking pot when you stop smoking cigarettes."

"But Billy. What you're doing is illegal. You're breaking the law."

"To be honest with you Nicole, there is nothing I would rather do than smoke a big fat joint right now."

THE ESCAPIST

"Fuck you. I'm leaving. I'm not dating no criminal."
"Nicole, wait. Wait. Wait! Don't leave. Please stay. Sit down. Sit your ass down Nicole! Nicole! Nicole!"

Left with your own thoughts in an empty hotel room. And yes, Nicole just broke up with you. A lot of your stash, confiscated. Just got out of a fucking jail cell.

Something.
The final straw:
You were home for part of the summer after your first year at Mission Mountain. Dad got you to go to the gym with him. You went, but you hated every second of it. Mainly because you had to see him naked in the locker room. And he always made you get naked too. Something about being a man. On the way home, you and Dad stopped into Dunkin Donuts. You were going to get a cup of coffee, bagels, too. You saw her standing in line a few people ahead of you. Melanie Rae. Your sweetheart from Tompkins. The first girl you had sex with. You were 15 when you and her first did it, in her brother's bed while her parents were in the kitchen. You looked at Dad and told him you wanted to leave. He didn't understand—you had just walked in.

--Look, you whispered.
You nodded your head in her direction.

--Oh. What's the big deal.
--Dad, I really want to get the fuck out of here.
--Stand your ground, Little Shrimp.

Red cheeks. Sweat. You couldn't help but to look at her. She was with some toolbag. Her latest in a long line of other toolbags that came before him. Laughing. Smiling. It was overpowering. Please don't look back. Please don't look back at me, you thought.

--Dad, what if she looks back here?

--Stand your ground, Shrimp. Stand tall, he whispered back.

--What the fuck difference does it make if I'm standing tall? I don't want to be in this fucking Dunkin Donuts anymore. Can we please just get the fuck out of here?

--Watch your language, Shrimp! he yelled. You think these people want to listen to you cursing all day? Have some manners!

Melanie Rae turned around at this point and was staring at you, laughing uncomfortably. The toolbag was staring and laughing too. You were flushed. You walked right on out of there. As you were walking out, you overheard him say something to her:

--No respect. I don't blame you for dumping his sorry ass.

You kicked the tire of a car parked outside of Dunkin Donuts. It really hurt. You decided to walk home. That was when you told yourself you never wanted to see him again. Then you packed up your stuff and went back early to Mission Mountain. Funny it was that that was the final straw.

THE ESCAPIST

But you did want to see him again. It was about three years later when Cynthia called you when she found out Dad would be returning home. This would be his last tour of duty. His days of acting as medic had come to an end. Purple Heart. A lot had changed since he left. You finally moved the hell away from there and to the big city. You had found a listing for a shitty basement apartment on Craigslist and went for it. You were finally out on your own, and you stopped wetting the bed.

You secured a job in the mailroom at a big skyscraper of a building in midtown. You rode the train every morning, and it felt good to ride the train. When you went back home to Baltimore to check in on Cynthia and bring her her meds, it was like an empty shell of what it had once been. He was gone. Peter was gone. She was also like an empty shell, and that's the way she liked it. You and her both.

You drove Cynthia to the airport to pick him up. Both sober for the moment. She asked you if you were nervous. You told her of course you were nervous. Cynthia found out Dad's terminal and you both waited for him right past the security gate. Travelers were passing by you in a whirlwind, circling and spinning with all that luggage and all the happiest emotions in the world on display as they embraced their loved ones: hugging, squeezing, kissing, laughing, cuddling, smiling, handholding. You couldn't help but stare.

Then there he was. Back from the dead. He was wearing the navy-blue suit with the ribbons down his breast. His body was now sculpted into a smaller fitter form than how you remembered. Dad's outer layer of fat and muscle had vanished. There was an eye patch covering the non-existent right eye and a long scar stretching from his forehead up his scalp and down past his right ear. He looked like a warped version of himself. Like an odd breed. Dad and Cynthia embraced first. He stared blankly at you with his one eye while Cynthia copied those around her by attacking the man she loved with affection. She inspected him, his scar, then planted a number of kisses all over his face. How nice that would be. To be kissed like that. To be loved like that. But Dad just took it.

He held out his hand for you. You put out your hand, and he gave it a power-grip and pulled you in quickly knocking your body into his. You could smell his BO. He'd been on three different planes within the last thirty-five hours.

It took close to forty-five minutes to drive back to Dundalk. Dad was fast asleep in the front seat a few minutes after pulling out of the parking lot.

He opened the door to your childhood home. He raised you and Peter here just like Grandma and Grandpa did for him and Uncle George. The stench of stale cigarettes was in the air, but Cynthia had cleaned up in honor of his arrival. Blankets were neatly folded over the sofas, rugs vacuumed, the kitchen counters sparkling, the magnets and pictures on the refrigerator aligned perfectly next to each other.

He didn't feel like talking. Just tired from flying for a day and a half is what Cynthia said. But you knew that he just wasn't the same person anymore. All in the span of a few years. He had seen his mates blown to bits probably. Probably had his fingers inside of them too. How many was he actually able to

THE ESCAPIST

save? Did he save anybody?

How can you expect someone to be the same person they were after going through that—after fighting a war on another planet? How can anyone expect you to go back to your old life, your old fucked life? She expected it. She was sorely mistaken.

You secretly wanted it too. Why would you want that? But you did want it. He'll never touch you again.

PART TWO

10

Billy slept until one in the afternoon, past the hotel's checkout time, and woke to the housekeeper walking in. Nicole and all of her belongings were gone. He quickly packed up his things, walked straight past the front desk and continued through South Beach to get to his car. Along his walk he called Macy and got the name of her lawyer, Brad McMannus-Evans Esquire, and was able to set up an appointment. His secretary told him that the soonest Mr. McMannus-Evans would be able to see him was Thursday at noon. He needed some time to gather information about the case. Billy pleaded with her to be seen before that—he was ready to leave this city, this state—but she persisted that that was the soonest.

He plopped down on the beach half way through his walk. He took off his t-shirt and pants even though it was a bit windy and lay down on the sand in his boxer briefs. He soaked his pale white skin in the sun until it started to burn. When it started to burn, he got into the cold water. He dragged his feet against the current until he was deep enough to drop his body underwater. It shocked his system when he dropped down into the ocean, and he liked it. The sensation went rapidly from his balls to his belly to his nipples to his neck to his face, until all the hair follicles were submerged. He held his breath and stayed down, opened his eyes, which stung from the salt, and then he shot back up out of the water. His body got adjusted to the temperature soon enough, and he drifted his way out farther. Each step closer to the horizon seemed to be the right step, and each step toward land seemed to be wrong. He continued until there was no more ground to walk on, and he was left idling in the water doing the dead man's float, the ocean pushing his body up to the sky and the sun's rays fighting back and pushing him back down to Earth, and he was bobbing, as close to floating as possible, between two realms, in the milky way, the barren abyss of space, a speck upon the nothingness of the universe, until the ocean decided to keep him by flipping him over with one of its large waves. It tumbled his body back to Earth. He choked and coughed, and instinctively, like a child crawling frantically to his mother, did the doggy paddle back to shore.

He stood at the edge of the ocean catching his breath and then air-dried his body until the goose bumps tingled all over. He was dry but wanted that shock from the cold again. He went back in, submerged his body, but it wasn't as good as the first time. He knew it wouldn't be.

After washing off in the public showers at the far edge of the beach, he gathered back up his things and continued on to find his car. He walked across the sands in a meditative state. Being in the sun, riding the crest of the ocean, hearing the waves, feeling the pull of the moon, hearing nothing else except for the chirps of the seagulls as if in his breast—it was a natural remedy, even though it was short-lived. *If only this, all of this, right now, could be crumpled up, shrunk down, melted down into a pill-sized capsule to be ingested every morning after waking up.*

He stopped for a late lunch and then later for a drink, and when he finally reached the Nissan, he threw his bag into it and then saw the $120 parking ticket on the windshield. It didn't strike a cord with him, like it was supposed to be there. Like it was part of the grand scheme of things, part of the chaos of the universe. He got into the car, rolled his seat back into a reclining position, opened his journal, yet before he could write anything, he dozed off.

He woke hours later—vivid dreams interrupted by loud random noises from outside the car. He wished for tinted windows. He opened back up his journal and saw he had written something:

Sweaty as hell. Dreaming. There was a tall muscular man with octopus arms and a long face. It was the face of your father.

He tried to remember writing it. He must have been half asleep. There was a sudden tapping on the window. A short man in uniform was tapping with his pointer finger. It was light out, but Billy had no idea what time it was. "You can't park here," he heard him say through the fogged up glass.

"Sorry," he yelled back, startled, disoriented.

Billy took off. He felt hunger pangs, but those were interrupted by the psychological compulsions that began directing his actions. The need to feed this more immediate craving triumphed over the need for food.

A lot of it was taken from him. He felt exposed. His hands gripped tight around the steering wheel as he tried to think logically about what he could do to replenish his stash, and he was quick to rationalize that a good binge on a portion of what he had left in the cooler to appease the immediate need would bring about the solution. He reached down into it, dosed, and while the narcotics were working their way into his bloodstream, he circled around Miami for almost an hour before stopping outside of a diner called Paradise, adjacent to a gas station. He went into the gas station first and bought a pack of cigarettes and a six-pack of beer. He took it back to the car and drank quickly and efficiently. It helped to temporarily settle his nerves. He stepped out and smoked a few cigarettes and walked in circles around the car.

Returning to the driver's seat and leafing through his journal, he suddenly felt like he was just a heap of skin and bones holding in place a frenzied mind with rapidly discharging synapses firing off in all directions, one high-speed tangential trail of thought after another. He read his very last entry, and then he put pen back to paper.

Why did this long-faced father with octopus arms come to you in your dreams? Just don't know. Maybe the long-faced father with octopus arms didn't actually come to you in your dreams. Maybe he just came to you as your pen was making contact with paper.

Maybe you wrote it because dreams are pretty interesting. Dreams are an escape from all this. Maybe you should start writing them all down. That would make Felix so happy, he'd go into a tailspin.

Maybe you decided to write it down to feed this lie to yourself that you actually have something interesting to say about a man with octopus arms, an interesting story to tell. Was this you trying to be clever and interesting by concocting a creature that would conjure up certain thoughts and emotions in potential readers, i.e. strangers who you'd hope would secretly read it after inconspicuously leaving the journal in plain sight? Strangers that could see that you had fascinating dreams about mythological beings, that you were a prodigy with an inexplicable mind, not some defective less-than-average waste-of-space nothing?

Is it possible the long-faced father with octopus arms truly did come to you in your dreams? You may never know. Or you can keep questioning now, on the page. Continue the search here. Continue to write. For more reasons. For peace. You don't meditate. You don't do that yoga shit. Maybe that's why you're writing this in the first place—to meditate through words, to make some sort of discovery, to find a reason to live.

Was it written to sustain survival? To not give up the struggle? And in your sleep, were your dreams telling you to survive? Perhaps your unconscious self had realized that there was always a choice and that if you wanted to write about a long-faced father with octopus arms, you were free to do so, and if you wanted to fill your belly with digoxin, you were free to do that too. Were your true intentions to show yourself that writing it down just complicates as opposed to clarifies? That the only clarity is that death can come as easily as a sudden jerk of the wheel?

For now, you're alive, so your nerves are still working in the way they were designed—toward survival. Will the time come when the synapses start to malfunction? Perhaps their malfunction has already begun. And thus you're dying.

Good.

But you've made yourself clear on one thing—that you don't know. It says a lot about someone. Someone that says they do not know. You don't know why the long-faced father with octopus arms came to you in your dreams. It's like you have no idea what the fuck you're talking about. Just spitting out useless bullshit and hoping for some sort of configuration of meaning or a deeper understanding of reality or some sub-reality, or some understanding of your fucked-up psyche that you'll be able to wrap your thoughts around and be interested in and care about and they'd care about you. He'd care about you. He'd say that he was sorry. He'd say that he loves you.

But maybe he shouldn't matter anymore. Let him perish. Maybe it's the image that matters. Maybe you gotta just follow that image, document where it goes and what it does as it all becomes apparent to you. But if you follow it, will you just be digging a deeper and deeper hole for yourself? A six-foot hole to bury yourself in. But saying that you don't know...Can you gain anything from that or will it just coerce you closer to the clarity of death? Can you start with that and then prove to write something of value, be something of value? Just don't know. And didn't know when sitting down to write this. That brings you full circle then. God, look at you.

11

Billy staggered into Paradise diner, relieved himself in the bathroom, washed his face and under his armpits, and then took a seat in a booth with his journal in hand.

"Pizza's half off, sweetheart," said the waitress as she was walking by his booth. Billy realized she was speaking to him and he looked up at her as she was passing, and it was a majestic moment. It was her dark olive complexion and her slender body, her flowing locks of hair all the way down to where her apron was tied around her back, but mostly it was her little smile. She was happiness.

"Let's do it to it…I'll take a Bud, too, " he said.

"You got it, sweetheart," she said as she walked back into the kitchen.

He liked being called sweetheart. And there was something genuine in the way she said it. *You are a sweetheart, aren't you?* In the booth across from him he watched a large man with bushy sideburns and a receding curly fro chew away at his pizza. It made Billy reconsider ordering it after watching him eat.

"How you doin' Dougie?" the waitress called to the man in the booth next to him when she popped back out of the kitchen.

"Just fine, Bernice. Thanks. I'll take another Coke, though, please and thanks." Then the man made small murmurings to himself. He glanced at Billy and resumed eating his pizza.

Billy opened his journal. He flipped through and read back to himself what he had recently written while crossing out certain sentences and words.

He looked back up at the man in the booth across from him and watched as his pointer finger and middle finger slid under the pizza crust while the thumb clamped down on top. The man raised the slice into the air and shimmied his other hand underneath the base of it before the cheese and sauce could drip off onto the table. The tip of the slice rested on the arch of his palm, and he brought it forth to his cavernous mouth. His tongue rolled out to accept the slice and worked in unison with his hands to course it deep into the dark crevice of his mouth. His teeth chomped down quickly, once, twice, three times, a fourth time. He brought what was left of the slice back to his mouth with force and wiggled it in producing a buildup of red sauce around the corners of his lips—chewed and swallowed. The remaining crust got tossed onto the plate and joined the other pieces of crust that were now mounted up like piles of bones.

You were thinking about making conversation with Dougie, the large man across from you with the pizza sauce-covered mouth, but you didn't want to disturb the animal while it was feeding—a tall meaty sort of fellow with double chins and a big puffy head of hair over his long forehead. He looks almost like an adult version of your old roommate at Mission Mountain, Simi. Simi was big, too, like this guy, had the double chins, the big head of curly hair, just no facial hair yet. Simi, with his bad lisp. He made the shh sound for his esses. When Simi would pass you around the halls and grounds, he would sing out something that sounded like "tippy, tippy, tip," out of the corner of his lips while doing a comical jig.

--What's up Simi, you would say while pretending to be amused by his antics.

He'd stick out his hand for a high five and you'd usually return the favor, or sometimes you'd have a nice goofy handshake together that would last for five seconds too long. As he'd dance off after he'd give his salutations, you'd turn around and look at him and watch as he hot-stepped away—danced away, not walked away, but danced—as if his only concern regarded what was going to be served for dinner.

You and Simi used to walk to dinner together, walk through Corridor K, which encircled Mission Mountain—Corridor L was a lot shorter of a walk than Corridor K, but you always liked taking the long walk. Simi didn't care. On Corridor K before dinner you could watch as the sun was setting, its last remnants still coming in through the windows along the corridor, ricocheting off of the steel walls and illuminating the dust particles. Simi's head would just be to the ground, staring at his feet as they shuffled past one another.

After dinner, the two of you would take Corridor L back to the room. You'd kick off your shoes and climb up onto the bed. You spent so much time just lying there. Just mulling over how you were going to fulfill your next craving. You wrote it all out on sticky notes. You had them placed all along the wall next to your bed. You must have had fifty of them placed all over it, in no particular pattern, just randomly placed up and down, left and right of the wall. You learned the chemical compounds for the drugs—science class did prove useful—used the chemical formulas so no one knew what you were writing about. It was your secret code, indecipherable to Simi, to any of the superiors that saw them. $C_{21}H_{23}NO_5$—morphine alkaloid, heroin. $C_{22}H_{28}N_2O$—condensed carboxamide, fentanyl. $C_9H_{13}N$—amphetamine.

Simi usually didn't talk to you after meals; he usually just climbed into bed and fell asleep, like an ape. Not always though.

--Hey, I shee you...shooo shchemey. You're shooo shchemey, he said to you once, looking at you writing out your stickies.

--Why is that Simi, you said without looking over.

--You're shtarbing yourshelf to make it look like youuur shick. You know the shpeshial treatment they give the shick kidsh."

--Nah, I just don't want to eat that nasty day-old crap they serve us.

He would fall asleep and you would receive the pleasure of listening to his snoring grunts and moans. You learned to live with him though—it actually wasn't that difficult once you were able to tune out the sound of his conversations with himself, his mammoth size, and his loud snores. Eventually, you became accustomed to the sound of his snores. They became almost hypnotic. They would carry you away into a sweet dream, at first anyway.

Innocent Simi. Simi wasn't one of the bad ones. But it was like he wasn't bothered by anything. Maybe he just didn't have the capacity to be bothered by anything, by anyone or anything that had anything to do with school or with the outside world. And that was good for you. He, like you, didn't have any family that came to visit. He was terrible in class, tried but just couldn't get any of it. But bitterness? None whatsoever. You never saw his lips become anything less than a straight line. Having a straight face wasn't even common—he was always smiling or giggling about some minute sensory perception, or something of even lesser value.

There was that one morning you woke up super early, way before the morning bell. It was still dark outside. Simi's snores still circulated throughout the room. You remembered that dream you had. Still remember it now. And you stuck a bunch of stickies together and wrote out what happened—and maybe that's why you still remember it now—you had wings on your back, and you could fly. You could soar through the sky. And you flew over the ocean, skimming the water, and you got caught in this net of immortality in the middle of the sea. You were dragged into the depths but your abnormal lung capacity kept you alive. You were brought into an underworld where you faced weird demons and evil sea monsters of all sizes, but they couldn't kill you. But you were trapped as a prisoner there underwater forever, never able to fly again. Then you added the stickies to the wall. You sorted through other stickies. Did some new ones. Threw out old ones.

And it was at breakfast, maybe a day, maybe a week, maybe a month after that, and you were sitting next to Woog in the cafeteria. How many times was it that you and Woog doped together. He was there the first time. Him and Stevo—Stevo was the one who first pushed the needle in for you at that playground a few blocks from Mission Mountain, the one who showed you how to do it. The gatekeeper. So you were sitting with Woog at breakfast—you two never really talked much to each other at breakfast, but all he had to do was just give you that look which meant he had it, then you'd go do it. He would otherwise just eat with his face down at his food, not willing to look up unless he heard gunshots or something.

--Did Simi make a move on ya yet? Woog murmured with his eyes still in his cereal bowl. He looked as if he had asked his Frosted Flakes if Simi had made a move on them...if Simi had made a move on each individual flake. But in reality, the question was directed toward you.

Woog spoke to his cereal again: Mihos...Mihos told me that Simi tried to kiss him. Yup, Simi likes the D.

You never even thought that Simi could know about that stuff. But Simi had feelings just like everyone.

--What the hell are you talking about, Woog? Mihos told you that?

--Mihos...Mihos told me that...Simi probably wanted to be

your roommate cause he wants a piece of you, too.

You left Woog and went back to your room. Then your mind went to places about that poor blubbering idiot. You wondered if he had a huge cock and if fucking Simi would be like fucking a horse. And it made you angry.

And the bad thoughts came in. The intrusive scene played out in your head, lying in bed there in the middle of the night. Still remember it: You took your sheet off your bed and ripped it down into strips, went over to Simi and tied both hands to the far bedpost while he was snoring. Tied the legs together and then tied them to the other end of the bedpost. Pulled his pants down and were right about the monstrous penis. Bigger than your arm. And you wanted to stop, that you couldn't do it, but you needed to get him before he got you. So you shoved globs of sheet into his mouth. And Simi opened his eyes. Saw himself in his predicament. Stared at you. Straight face. No frown, no smile, just a straight face. A confused face. It's was all very confusing. Still is.

Then, the bad scene continued in your head, and you couldn't stop it. You called him a fucker and hit him over and over on the head with your fist. Stopped and shoved more sheet into his mouth. Wrapped it around his head a couple of times. Pulled your pants down and got behind him in bed.

Then you steadied yourself and unwrapped the sheet around his head and removed it, untied his arms. And he was just panting with sweat and drool dripping down on his shirt and bed. You untied the other arm. Yet with both hands free, he still didn't untie his legs. With one hand he cupped his testicles and penis and with the other, he rubbed his head. You untied his legs. Simi was in this state of disorientation. Like you were. Like you always are.

--Hit me you fucking fuck, you saw yourself saying to him. Get up, hit me! Maybe it's cause you hated your brain for dreaming up the scenario in the first place.

You socked him in the face. Then again. Just as you knew how it felt. He pushed you back with his head to the ground.

--That's it, you fucking low life, you piece of shit, you saw yourself saying while punching him a third time. HIT ME!

As you threw punch number four, you saw something finally trigger deep down within him— he jumped out of bed and ripped you to the ground as if you were weightless. He whapped you open-handed over and over again. He cuffed you in the face and neck and head repeatedly. Cause that's what you wanted.

But then he was just there as before, as always, sleeping in his bed, snoring. Who really knows how Simi felt about you. Who knows if he ever actually did make a move on Mihos. But you couldn't be his roommate anymore. That was for sure. You put in a request for a new room. Soon enough you were bunked with Stevo. Back to doing new sticky notes and throwing away the old ones.

12

The diner was practically empty by the time he got up to leave. Dougie, the man in the booth across from him, had long since left, and there was an empty cup of coffee sitting at Billy's table, which he had nursed for the last hour while he was writing. He left a large tip for Bernice, for allowing him to stay, for calling him a sweetheart. He walked back to his car in the parking lot and drank the few remaining lukewarm beers before reclining his seat and wrapping himself in his sleeping bag. He read back through his journal, starting at the beginning. He reread what he had just written at Paradise Diner. A heavy and uncomfortable lump came in his throat for exposing himself so nakedly on the page. It had been so long, he had almost forgotten what it felt like. He eventually dozed off while a radio host spoke to him in a language he was unfamiliar with.

The next morning Billy went back to the diner—Bernice was there again—and he drank numerous cups of coffee with extra cream and extra sugar, had eggs and toast, then washed up in the bathroom before leaving. He left another nice tip for her. She smiled at him as he walked out. He smiled back. He glanced up at the clock on the wall and saw that he had to hurry to make it in time to the office of Brad McMannus-Evans Esquire for his noon appointment. On the drive over he felt optimistic about putting this episode behind him.

Billy found the address after circling around the neighborhood for a few minutes, pulled into the driveway and saw that it was a nice home-office overlooking the water. Billy walked right in, and Mr. McMannus-Evans was waiting for him behind his desk. He was wearing a suit and tie, was balding with glasses.

"William Chute?" the lawyer asked.

"Call me Billy."

"Ok, Billy. Take a seat young man. I'm sorry you've fallen into this mess."

"Yup, I'm a fucking idiot."

"Now, now, this could have happened to anyone. And it could have been a lot worse. Now, you have an arraignment scheduled to take place in two weeks, and the trial, if there is one, will take place sometime shortly thereafter."

"Fuck."

"Don't worry, the arraignment isn't a big deal. It will not be necessary for you to talk at the arraignment—you leave that to me. You will have to attend, however, as per the papers I will file today."

"An arraignment in two weeks? Then a trial? But I'm leaving today. I'm traveling."

"Where are you going? Back to Baltimore?"

"How do you know about Baltimore?"

"I saw that your residence is in Baltimore, no?"

"No…well, yes. It's where I grew up, but that's not where I live."

"Ok, well, where are you heading?"

"It's not important."

"Well, you'll have to be here for the arraignment and for the trial, granted there is a trial—only if they bring about a formal charge at the arraignment."

"I have to be here for all of this?"

"Unfortunately, yes."

"Shoot."

"Do you need a place to stay? We know of some very nice hotels that offer discounts for extended stays."

"What kinds of discounts?"

"$50 or $60 a night or so."

Billy arched his back straight and wiped imaginary soot from the sides of his shirt. "So, tell me, please, how are you going to handle this? What do we want to have happen?"

"We want them to throw this case out. Do you know how many pending cases there are right now clogging up the state's system? Cases hundreds of times worse than yours. A first time offender like you? A little bit of pot…a few prescription pills…please. They got bigger fish to fry. In any event—"

"Wait, I haven't even paid you yet."

"I understand, but I am willing to take the first steps for you, before any money. You understand, this is just my procedure. Once you're signed on as my client, I will first ask the state to provide a full discovery, which for all intents and purposes requires them to inform me of their entire case against you. I will then look over the discovery and will start discussions with the state to see what I can arrange as a plea offer, pointing out any and all deficiencies in their case. Unless I find a technical or legal fault in their case, which would warrant a motion to dismiss, I will be seeking a plea that would result in a dismissal of the case upon your satisfactory completion of a 'program,'" he finger-gestured with slouched shoulders. "With the filing of these papers you may receive something regarding that in the mail."

"As you know, I won't be able to receive. I'm traveling," Billy repeated.

Billy dropped his head into his hands.

"That's fine. Just fine. I'll be able to handle it on my end. I'll have them send it to my office here for you."

"Good…good." *Oh, Cynthia.* "So, how long is this going to take, really?"

"After the arraignment? Time frames are hard to judge this early in the case. I don't know if the state is going to be cooperative in providing the discovery in a timely basis or not. In any event, often times, delays work in your favor, such as witnesses resigning or relocating and not being available to the state, thus resulting in an inability for the state to prove its case, or a better plea offer. Therefore, we often use this as a tactic."

Billy stood up. "I just want to leave this fucking city. I am done with this place." He paced around the room, and Mr. McMannus-Evans watched with a convincingly sympathetic frown.

"If you leave," said Mr. McMannus-Evans, "you'll just have to come back in two weeks anyway, and then you may have to come back again if and when the state decides to move forward with your case. Trust me, we'll get you out of this. No problemo. Oh and one other instruction. Do not discuss this matter with anyone outside my office or sign any papers that do not come from my office without my personal instructions. I don't want you to make an incriminating statement that may be used against you in court, if this does end up going to court, which isn't likely. Just never waive attorney/client privilege or in any way unintelligently hurt your case."

"Fine. Fine. Fuck. How much is this going to cost me?"

"Initial retainer is twenty five hundred."

"What about after the retainer?"

"Expenses after all is said and done will be an additional one thousand."

Fuck me. Billy signed the contract. It happened so

quickly. The pen found its way into his hand, and Billy looked on as his hand wrote out his signature. He made a direct deposit from his checking account into Mr. McMannus-Evan's account to pay for the retainer. It drained much of his life savings, and he knew that if he didn't secure more money he would be in the red when the time for expungement came about. *Broke again, and stuck in Miami. You have enough gas left in the car to get you out of town, but what then?*

As he got back in the Nissan he sunk into his seat—gravity was pulling hard—the sinking brought on by the realization that he wasn't leaving Miami anytime soon, that all his money was vanishing, that his stash was low, that certain sacrifices would have to be made. He looked around his vehicle, caressed the steering wheel. *You're going to need to say goodbye. If Dad is going to be nomadic then you will be as well. If he's traveling on foot, then goddammit you can too.*

It was a rash decision, but he needed the money and felt that it was his only option. After sleeping in the car for another consecutive night, he started the ignition and drove to a McDonalds and ordered at the drive-through window. He sat in the parking lot and ate his breakfast sandwich and hash browns and spotted a dumpster in the back of the lot. He drove over to it after he finished eating and threw out many of his belongings, only keeping what he thought he was going to need: his pack, where he put his remaining pill bottles and baggies, phone charger, a few changes of clothes, his boots, basic toiletries, books of sentimental value, his journal, pens, and Swiss-Army Knife. He kept his sleeping bag, which he tied onto his pack, but the cooler and everything else, save for Bubba, was tossed. He cleaned the car out as best he could and rolled all the windows down to air it out. He drove around in circles looking for a used car dealership, which was much easier to find than he had anticipated. He found one within minutes—this was Miami after all.

And before he knew it, it was gone, and he felt truly alone. It had been his closest comrade for all of his young adult life. He got below the Blue Book value for it, but he was ok with it. He was ready to walk anyway. He decided that after the legalities were straightened out, he would travel by bus. *Just like Dad.* He sold the car to the dealership with the stipulation that the salesman drive him to wherever it was that he would need to go. The salesman was fine with the idea; it actually helped with his negotiations.

"Within reason of course," the salesman said. "We'll travel in style. We'll take the Firebird Convertible 400 H.O. Look at that beaut. Black interior, convertible top, hood tach, sexy stripe down the side. Rally IIs with trim rings, chromed to perfection rims. You give me the

Altima for eleven fifty, cold cash, and we'll cruise around in that sexy beast, and I'll take you wherever you need to go."

Billy shook on it. He used the bathroom at the dealership and changed into clothes that didn't smell as bad as what he had been wearing. He ran his hand down the side of the Nissan, kissed his hand and then gave the kiss to the car, said "thank you," and then got into the Firebird with the salesman. "Breakups are hard," Billy said as the Firebird was rolling out of the dealership.

First stop: Brad McMannus-Evans Esquire and Associates. Billy ran in, asked to speak with his lawyer and paid in full.

"Here's the rest of the money I owe you." He counted it out into a wad and dropped it down onto the table. There were a handful of large crisp bills left, and he put them back into his pocket. "Now you do your part and get me out of this mess."

"We'll take care of you, son. Just be sure I can get in touch with you when I need to. Keep your phone by your side. And don't go too far. I would assume you know how unwise it would be to leave the country. If you try leaving, they'll throw you right back in jail. After this case is settled, you can go anywhere you'd like."

Billy shook the lawyer's hand, thanked his secretary who gave him a paper receipt for the payment and a copy of the new contract, and he got back into the Firebird. Next and last stop: Paradise Diner.

✕ ✕ ✕

He sat down in the booth at Paradise, and Bernice brought him a coffee, extra cream, extra sugar, without asking. She smiled and dropped down a menu. As he was flipping through it, the sinking feeling returned, this time from selling off his best friend. *So, this is what it feels to mourn.*

"What would you like today, sweetheart?"

"Coffee is fine for me—thanks."

As Bernice was walking away, Billy called her back to his booth.

"Actually, I did want to ask you something: I'm looking for a cheap place to stay for a little while. Know of anything?"

"Yes, I know of a few places. How much are you looking to spend?"

"As little as possible."

"You know, I've seen a place a few blocks down from here that I think is a hostel. I remember seeing a sign on the front of the house. It doesn't look like anything special—I'm sure it's pretty cheap. Just go down 28th Street here, take a right on 27th Avenue, and you'll be there. It's the white house right on the corner. It's got a big blue wraparound porch."

"Perfect."

After a few more cups of coffee, Billy paid and left another good tip, to keep Bernice's good impression of him. He grabbed his pack wrapped with his sleeping bag and used Bubba to hoist himself up from the booth. He crossed the busy intersection, and after walking six blocks on 28th Street, he came upon it. It was just as Bernice had described, but the white paint was chipping off the sides of the house, and it had a rickety staircase and porch. He entered the house, and in the front office was a man with super thick glasses which magnified his eyes, and the man blinked at him. The man spoke quietly without making eye contact again. Billy paid for a night, and the man showed him to his bed. The room he was given only had a few other beds in it, none occupied, and they kept it pretty clean. The room had a back room space with lockers and a shower stall. Billy locked up his belongings and took a hot shower. The showerhead was low on the wall, and he had to duck his head down in order to wash.

When Billy went back into his room to dry off, someone was there sitting on one of the beds, seemingly waiting for him.

"Oh, hi there—I didn't see you come in! I'm Gabriel." He was short and skinny, about Billy's age or just a little older, no more than twenty-two or twenty-three years old, with tightly fitting stretchy jeans and a black sleeveless shirt. Gabriel sprawled onto his side on the bed resting his head on his hand, and Billy saw he had a tattoo of a dog with three heads on his bicep. His hair was parted and slicked back.

"Hello…"

"So, I'll just say this up front: if you're interested, it's fifty." Gabriel then ran his hand down his body as if it were a prize. "But if you want to have a fun night, it'll cost you extra."

"Wait, what?"

"Well, that's why you're here right? Hold on, let me start over. Again, my name is Gabriel, just looking to have a little fun. You're here to have a little fun too right?"

"No, I'm not looking to have any fun."

Billy walked back into the side room with the showers. He dried off quickly and put on a change of clothes. He walked back into the room, and Gabriel was gone, as if what had just transpired was a figment of his imagination.

He walked over to the laundromat across the street to finally wash his clothes and his sleeping bag. *Fresh start.*

Billy returned to Paradise Diner that evening for dinner. It was more crowded with most of the booths occupied, and Bernice was acting especially friendly with many of them. It stung. When she would walk back in his direction, he would stare up at her to hopefully make eye contact and exchange another smile. He watched as she attended to the customers, and he was in awe of a certain elegance that she exuded; she was the mistress of her domain. She knew exactly how to speak to them, could already know what they were going to order as if reading their faces or would be immediately prepared for any kind of request they would throw at her. She would reach into her apron and grab a straw to place on the table just as a patron was about to ask for an extra one. She would drop some napkins down on the table as some ketchup would smudge onto a patron's face.

As she approached from the other end of the bar, right before a possible contact with Billy, she was called over to another young lady in a booth on the other side of the diner. They were laughing with one another; Billy assumed they were friends. Bernice rested her left foot behind her right one and had her hand on the shoulder of the other woman. Billy stood and walked over to the bar, leaned against it to pretend to be watching the news on the small television on the wall but really wanted to listen in on their conversation. He caught the tail end of it and heard that the two of them and another coworker of hers were planning to go to a place that sounded like Switchback Bar after her shift ended. Billy glanced away from the television, and as she walked past him, Billy smiled. Bernice gave a smile back, and it was just enough for Billy to not lose hope. He returned to his booth and had already made up his mind about what his next course of action would be. He would follow her to Switchback Bar to see her outside of the diner setting, to try to do the unthinkable and actually get such a pretty girl like Bernice to like him.

Later that evening, back at the hostel, Billy rolled up a small pinner, smoked it on the street corner quickly, went back in, waved to the man that ran the establishment and told him that he was going out for the night. He walked back over to the diner and sat at the bench at the adjacent gas station and played on his cell phone until he saw Bernice walking out with her bag draped over her shoulder. She crossed the main intersection and walked east. Billy followed behind her to Switchback Bar a few blocks away and was casually and nervously going to bump into her and strike up a conversation on instinct and have it possibly pick up steam leading to drinks and then sweet lovemaking in positions he had only ever seen before online. Billy fantasized about fucking her up the ass, and he found it upsetting that he was letting his imagination run riot with this thought, that a deep-seeded repulsion was turning into temptation.

13

Billy entered Switchback Bar and took a seat at the other end of the bar from Bernice and her friends, ordered an IPA and a shot of Jameson, held his cell phone in his hand and pretended to be engaged with it in order to steal glances at his crush. With a cackling coming out of heavy-duty headphones, a man entered through the door and sat a few barstools down from him next to an apparent friend or at least an acquaintance, and they slapped hands which culminated into a crisp snap.

"Sup, Grove," the friend said to him.

"Chillin, dog."

Billy watched him closely as he ordered a Hennessy. Billy was immediately captivated by the confidence that just seemed to ooze out of him. He had tattoos weaving their way down his forearms seeping out of his loose fitting orange short-sleeved shirt. He was sporting a New York Yankees hat that still had the hologram sticker on the rim askew upon dreadlocked hair. Billy wondered if he was from New York or if he was merely a team enthusiast, or if perhaps his motives for wearing the hat were more about style.

Billy returned his stare to Bernice though circled his eyes back to Grove who was also playing with his cell phone, also now stealing glances at the young women around him. Billy saw Grove glance to his left, and Billy watched how Grove's eyes narrowed in on Bernice. *Target locked and ready for deployment.* Billy drank his beer in big gulps while tapping his fist on his twitching leg.

Grove was drawn in immediately, Billy could tell. Just as he had been. As were the other men, too, that were swarming around her. But Grove's method was more calculated, bolder, slicker than anything Billy could have come up with. Grove got off his barstool, no hesitation, slow-paced it up to her, and suddenly Billy felt the compulsion to get up as well. Billy followed in the same direction imitating Grove's swagger and then stopped suddenly when he saw how effortlessly Grove weaved through her circle of friends and slid into the open barstool next to her.

Billy heard Grove say to her, "Hey there pretty lady. Let me holla at you for a second pretty lady. Pretty lady let me be the little bird on your shoulder. Tellin' you sweet things on the living room sofa. Like your hair is spun silk and you got milky breasts. But for real I can't get over how you rockin' that dress…I confess that I've been watchin' you watchin' me watchin' you, it's impossible, but envisionin' you up in the hospital, having my kids, your beauty is a natural bliss, I capture your kiss, and now I'm like an addict with this."

The circle of friends had hushed down, and they were now listening in as well, in wonder, in amusement.

"It's never enough, the lust, tail feathers and such. I must grab ya, must have ya tender touch, wich' ya' slender butt, waist, hips, thighs and toes. I'm blinded though, cause love is like a mind control, a confinin' mold that's certainly been tried and sold. But I want you to be mine to hold and share with you my wine and dro. Oh, and a final note before we get too deep in this game, could you please just tell me your name?"

Shivers ran up Billy's spine during Grove's tirade; his words tickled Billy's brain. Bernice bobbed her face forward and back a few times with raised eyebrows and an awkward smile while it was happening, and by the end was laughing uncomfortably and stuck out her hand and greeted him appropriately.

"It's Bernice. Thanks for that, but I have a, uh, how about you just buy me a drink." She turned her eyes to her friends. "It's Kettle One and soda, two limes," she slipped out after pausing, blushing but hiding it well.

Grove looked across the bar in the other direction and shook his head as though realizing that she was about to play him and wasn't going to take this game seriously. Billy's method would have been to get her stoned and loose and to get her to fall for him while floating through a counterfeit paradise.

Billy couldn't remember the name of the third man but his appearance reminded him of a phlegm-filled spitball with a golden tint, and he liked the analogy and wanted to remember it to write down later. The third man sat at the bar next to Bernice on the opposite side of Grove and ordered a brandy on the rocks for himself "and whatever Bernice here wants." After purchasing her drink, the third man used other kinds of words from Grove's to seduce her, soft words into her ear, and Billy could only make out a little bit of it, but he knew that the words didn't rhyme like Grove's; he knew that they just smelled of money. Billy watched her get up from her barstool without saying another word to Grove, move to a corner table with the other man; a dim candle was lit and there was less noise to distract them. *Fine then. Go off and live your dream with your knight in shining armor.* They fell into their own bubble of gooey love, kissing and petting, and that was when Billy lost interest. The circle of friends petered away, and Billy took a seat on Bernice's barstool and felt the warmth her ass had left.

Grove and Billy sat silently, brought together by Bernice, yet both had lost the battle to the man with money in his pockets and shiny black shoes on his feet with a gleaming gel-smeared head of loafing hair. Grove had dark interlocking weaves of hair with what looked to Billy like intricate patterns plastered upon his head. Billy's: now a tumbleweed of brown and blond—something that started as an easy-to-manage buzz cut with slender sideburns clipped to a tip at the bottom of his earlobes. They both slowly nursed their alcoholic beverages.

"Not that I was spying or anything, but I liked what you had to say to her," Billy finally declared to Grove. "Too bad it didn't work," he continued. "A lot more creative than my method. But fuck that guy, and fuck her."

Indeed, Billy lost interest in wooing Bernice. Seeing her french kissing the other man was a sure sign to give up the effort. Billy's pursuit of Bernice died almost as quickly as it was born, and that night he gave up on it completely—he had gotten pretty good at starting things and quitting them—but this lead him to Grove, the man to his right, for his next ephemeral endeavor. For he was now running just as fast as ever up that disintegrating staircase to the sky, each step a new fleeting obsession to escape the previous one and all that preceded it. To get so high until gravity released its grasp.

Grove half smiled at Billy's candor and presented a couple small dimples, one on his cheek and the other cropped around the corner of his lips. He tipped the top of his beer slightly to the side simply as a lethargic way to hold his beer bottle. However, Billy thought this to be a toast and clanged his drink against his. "Cheers to freedom, aye?"

Finally Grove spoke. "Well, why didn't your method work?" he spattered out of the side of his mouth.

"Unfortunately, I didn't get a chance to actually try it out. You and Fancy Pants over there beat me to it."

Grove stared forward with glazed eyes at his reflection in the mirror on the other side of the bar with his back and shoulders comfortably arched downward.

"I'll let you in on a little secret—you can't hesitate," Grove said, still staring forward. "You just gotta act. You can't stop to think about it. If you doubt yourself, she'll see right through you. If you got any sort of self hang-up, it's a big fucking shit stain on your shirt. You'll be off. Your whole game goes down the toilet. The moment you sat down here I could tell you was a flake."

Under the bar in his lap, Billy popped open a small bottle of pills with the prescription label and black marker sketched over it, swallowed a small dose of his special formula into his system triggering a lip flinch and quick roll of the head.

"So those pills help you hit on women, then."

"They help me sit at this bar, they help me engage in conversations like these, they allow me to walk out the door in the morning…you want one?"

"Shit, I'll take two."

After getting past the angst of this first conversation, Billy latched onto Grove for the rest of the night, if only through a shared intoxication and to learn from Grove's pursuit for women. They headed out to a couple of other bars around the neighborhood and neither had much luck. Billy couldn't get any attention from women, while Grove didn't see anything he liked: women as soft objects that he could mold and contour into creations of his own. Grove stayed away from the freethinking types, as he called them, and much preferred young sporty girls whom he could easily operate and maneuver and coerce. As the night got later and later Billy developed more of a whatever-comes-my-way outlook—in fact, that had been his outlook from the beginning; however, his ego was slightly inflated for a short while just from being next to this monument of a man—but not even whatever-comes-my-way presented itself.

At this late hour, drunk and over-stimulated, Billy considered resorting to putting down some of the change left in his pocket for any sort of action, and as the alcohol and drugs continued to influence his thoughts and continued to convince him that what he was about to do was okay, that it was all going to be okay, he couldn't fight off the pull any longer, and by 3:40 in the morning, after last call and after exchanging phone numbers with Grove, he was back at the hostel. He walked in and after seeing that none of the beds were occupied, staggered over to the man in the front office who was reading a badly-creased book. Numbly, somberly, he asked, "Is Gabriel around?" The man pushed his thick glasses down to the base of his nose, tilted his head down and looked inquisitively into Billy's eyes. He then picked up the phone and made a call.

Billy knew he liked women, they still brought about those tingles in his genitals, but those small lusty excruciating cravings had crept back in even after he had thought he moved on and away from them, away from these things he thought he had burnt to dust with his father and the rest of his adolescence, locked away, thrown away the key, yet they had lingered back into his desirous mind by wearing a shadowy cloak over their shoulders late at night, in the dark, when no one was around to see. Billy walked into the room. He shut off the lights. After lying in bed for a short while with his head spinning in circles, he heard the voice: "I'm glad you changed your mind." As Gabriel undressed Billy, his eyes rolled into the back of his skull.

Thirty-five minutes later, he was alone, and his body was shaking as he passed out for the night. Soon after waking, he vomited violently into the toilet, then fell to the ground of the bathroom. While lying there, he told himself that he would never let the encounter slink back into his thoughts. When the bad thoughts came they were always fleeting anyway, always just momentary images of body parts and sweat, like forgotten dreams.

✕ ✕ ✕

Billy took a long hot shower, dressed, then removed all his belongings from the locker and walked over to Paradise Diner. Bernice said good morning, called him sweetheart as usual, and plopped down a cup of coffee on the table for him. She flashed her ubiquitous smile. *Why must you play this game?*

"How did that hostel work out?"

"Oh, it was fine. Thanks."

He knew he couldn't go back to it. He scrolled through his list of contacts in his cell phone and found Grove's phone number. Still unable to escape Florida for at least another two weeks, he needed a place to stay. Grove was a logical choice, a promising new friend.

"Good morning," Billy said when Grove answered his phone.

"Aight."

"How you feeling this morning?"

"I feel like sheeet, man. You zinged me last night."

"Welcome to the team."

"Word."

"It was real good to meet you, man."

"Okay."

"Want to do it again tonight?"

And the unlikely duo spent another night out together with the intention of finding women, but again, they had minimal success. Again, late into the evening, while sitting together at a dive in a stupor brought on by one of Billy's patented formulas, Grove mentioned that he had recently moved from Liberty City to Overtown.

"The real OGs are in Liberty, but my boy got a hook up in Overtown. We got soundproofed walls. A whole studio set up in the back. The place is legit."

"Close to Miami?"

"Damn close. You can see downtown from my window."

It was Billy's chance: "That's interesting you say that…because I'm looking for a place to stay for the next couple of weeks. Would you mind letting me crash with you? It would only be for a couple of weeks. I don't really have anywhere else to stay, and you know I'll keep hooking you up."

"Just a couple of weeks?"

"Yea, it all depends on my court case—but I'll be out as soon as it's over."

"And you'll keep hooking me up?

"I'll keep hooking you up."

"And my boys?"

"I'll hook them up too."

Grove consented, and Billy was in.

It only took a few days before Grove, which he learned was short for Grover, developed a few grudges against Billy, mainly about him being leachy, yet at the same time he enjoyed the partnership, as he benefited from Billy's free drugs. Billy never let on that his stash was running low, and fast. He was smart enough to recognize his role in the relationship yet still latched on to this other human being with everything he had, for Grove seemed to be his only friend in the world. Billy thought he was amusing to Grove with his addictive drug-induced psychoses, and he thrived off having the ability to readily distribute his narcotics among Grove and his crew. Just the thought of telling people who his best friend was withered within him!

"You know I think I *have* started to have some effect on you, I'm helping your rap game, expanding your ideas," Billy said to Grove. "Though you're not saying much to me, you *are* smoking my shit, dropping my opies. Your thoughts are starting to bend a little because of me, I think, right? And I think it's great because you've really affected me with everything, man. I mean, your lyrics are so damn amazing. I mean, listening to them makes me feel, like, alive, you know?"

Billy knew how powerful words could be; he had already fallen in deep with putting them to paper, thanks to Felix. He could relate to Grove because Grove also tried to verbalize his inner life, used them to try to tell a story. However, Grove's ability to spin words vocally, words that rhymed for that matter, was a true talent in Billy's mind, and he wanted to be a part of it, to live in it.

Grove acknowledged that this seeming clash of cultures was having an impact on Billy, but he had better things to occupy his time. In fact, Grove seemed pressed to find anything more than a couple of dark patches of camaraderie for his new roommate as the days passed. Billy could pick up on these dark patches, however, and he milked them for all they were worth—they gleamed like bright white blemishes on Billy's empty, sad soul. Grove's vibe entered Billy's veins, and he felt it deep; it was invigorating. It was clear that Grove knew how Billy felt about him and sometimes tried to be sympathetic to it while freestyling at random:

"You have no other recourse than to follow my forms with the fondlin' and fumblin' of a young foundlin'," he spit at Billy. "That is, you stumble along in darkness lookin' to shed your light from within…find a friend, find a foe, whose gonna help ya' grow—the help being your boy Grove and the blind little doe…that's you, Joe Schmo."

"You've put other words in me I never thought existed," Billy cracked back. "Starting now, right now, I make this promise to you—I'm going to flow like you. This is what I want. Time to make this flip, you planted a microchip." But Billy was not very good at keeping promises.

× × ×

Billy would lie on the floor in his sleeping bag in his temporary makeshift hallway bedroom and listen through the walls as Grove and his rapper friends were putting together a six-track demo, and while listening to its rhythmic resonance and putty-like words, Billy shunned himself for being nothing in a world of greatness. Billy's only place existed within himself.

Billy would look in the mirror and see white skin and that's what he was to them, he admitted, a white boy, a young lost white boy. Soon, Grove would be just a memory, just another record of Billy's failure at finding love.

While the thumping of bass and drum and the screaming of lyrics blasted through the walls, he considered that he didn't even know how to speak to Grove in the way he spoke and in the way his friends spoke and that when the time came to communicate, he couldn't mumble much more than a few sentences with the very man he was trying to emulate without him giving Billy a look of impertinence.

Billy embraced his nightlife with them, his time to try out his new ego. He tried to reinhabit the idea that at night it's harder to see people for whom they really are in the darkened shadows. You just see that shade of a man, that moving figure with no real attributes except their words which leave their hidden mouths to enter your ears for you to interpret, creating a character sketch in your mind of singular prominent elements—and you come to understand who they are and not whom they're trying to emulate. Billy tried to represent this new persona as much as he could when he was out late at night with Grove and his cronies, except his glossy whitened figure always seemed to break out, even when he didn't want it to, even in the dark; he couldn't help but let it break out.

Through all the alter egos that he would take on, through all the alter egos of his past, there was always one undeniable need that stayed with him. Not the drugs. No, something much bigger than that. Billy needed someone to love him. And someone that he could equally love back. Someone that could see him and into him, someone to find some sort of mutual understanding with him and for him to find the same. He would, time and time again throughout his life, ever since childhood actually, fantasize about having a twin—another Billy, always by his side for reciprocal and eternal comfort and companionship.

A week had passed, and in his temporary makeshift bedroom, Billy sobbed at night about not being able to find his footing in the world. Being with Grove brought it out of him. The loneliness made him quiver. Billy wanted others to see him for who he really was, even though he himself didn't even know. Could it finally emerge when Grove brought him into his world of flow? Fat chance.

But over the course of the following three days, he dedicated much of his time to writing one-liners and short rhymes in his journal and stopped looking back completely at his earlier entries. When his father and questions of his whereabouts would come back into his head, he blocked it out and focused on the task at hand, the new self.

When Thursday night arrived, only a few days before his arraignment, Billy was out walking the streets making a few quick deals, for he had a true knack for finding connects, and quickly—a talent that took years to master—and eventually he made his way back over to Grove's place, rang the buzzer and was let in, and he yelled "delivery!"

He disbursed the goods among Grove and his crew. He then sank into the couch in the living room and passed a bowl around. Grove's crew started jangling away there in the living room, all hyped up due to the excitement of it being close to the weekend. Billy decided to build up his courage and figured that now was his opening, his chance to try his hand at flowing. He panted heavily then stood up as Grove and two of his contemporaries, Donovan and Razor, were rapping over mix beats which Donovan had produced in the studio a couple of days earlier:

"These rap fools ain't got shit on this nigga," Donovan bellowed, "I'm the bigga figya' that ain't scared of the trigga', n' these wiggas is lily I shoot em' right in they backpack, with a black gat, the mic, shoulda' never've grabbed that…"

"Yea buddy, this shit 'bout to get ugly," roared Razor, "we run the underground just like the subway, n' trust me, these niggas don't want it wit Razor, I chew these fuckas up like Now N Laters…"

"Let me get at the mic," Grove piped in, "and tell these motha fuckas for real, they should study with zeal before this shit gets bloody in here, n' don't fear, you know this nigga stay in the cipha', that's right, I lock this shit down like a lifa'."

With his guts hanging out and his belly to the floor, Billy leaped into the circle and put forth his first and last real attempt at flow:

"I see y'all rappin' and I had to come, and see if y'all were having some fun. I'm white lightnin', I'm a really dope rapper. And no one's as good as me, I'm the master." *Breathe…Breathe.* "Catch me on the corner with a foreigner to our game, and I'll show 'em…"

Donovan, swiftly and with ease, clocked him one to the face, uttering something about knowing your place, and Billy went down to the ground quickly and stayed down. Then Donovan picked up from where he had left off.

Billy skulked out of the room, went to his makeshift bedroom and fought off the lump pushing its way up his throat causing him to gag. He removed a few different pills and threw them into his mouth. This pairing, he was familiar with it. It was a go-to. He took down his dosage with a dry gulp.

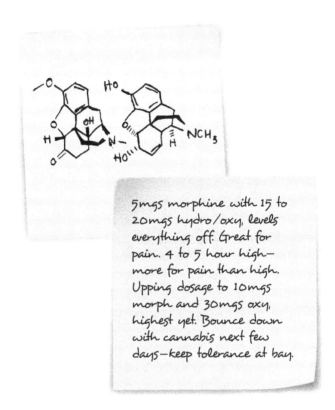

He stuck the sticky notes into his journal the next morning. Billy emerged from the hallway, he and Grove passed each other in the apartment, and Grove stared off in the other direction as Billy yearned for his glance, yearned for his attention. But Grove had bigger and better things to attend to, a rap game to pursue. There was no room in his world for Billy anymore, no interest in wasting more time with this wannabe who would just bring his game down, disrupt his flow.

14

Grove never explicitly told Billy to leave, but it was clear from Grove's blatant disregard for his presence that this friendship, or whatever it was, was over. For the last days leading up to the arraignment, Billy walked the city streets during the daylight, traveled north to go swimming and nap on the beach. He would quietly enter the home after dark, go to his sleeping area for the night and suffer through the blasting of music coming out of the living room, then leave again at break of day. The journal remained in his pack; he was perhaps uninspired, or more likely, the act of writing wasn't opening the pathways in the same ways anymore, in the ways Felix said they would. He was betraying the journal in the same way he felt betrayed.

On the morning of the arraignment Billy put on his cleanest outfit, an outstretched button-down with cargo pants, packed up his things, tied on his sleeping bag, grabbed Bubba, said goodbye to Grove who said "aight," and headed for the courthouse. He met Mr. McMannus-Evans outside of the building twenty minutes beforehand as he had been instructed to do over the phone the day before.

"Again, just let me do the talking," his lawyer said.

As they walked inside, Billy suddenly noticed the metal detectors of the courthouse and his legs became immobile. He slowly turned around and backed out of the building. His lawyer followed him outside, and they stood at the top of the stairs.

"What's the problem? You got the jitters?"

"That's one thing to call what I got. I can't go in."

"What do you mean you can't go in?"

"I mean I can't go in…with my pack."

"I see. Well it's a good thing you caught yourself this time. That would've been a double whammy, huh? The nightmare all over again." Mr. McMannus-Evans let out a little laugh, stopped and looked at Billy, then let out a louder one. Billy laughed too. Then they were both tittering with laughter. It had been too long since Billy had laughed like that, and with another human being. It was a comforting feeling, yet that was his lawyer's job, after all; that was part of the service for which Billy was paying.

"What should I do with it?"

"Let's throw it in my car. Let's hurry though, we don't want to be late."

After dropping his bag in his lawyer's Jag, they walked

quickly back into the courthouse. Billy double-checked all of his pockets for anything, anything at all that could get him in trouble like last time. He was sure he was clean and then walked through. He received a gentle pat down by a guard and was sent along. They walked up to the second floor where his arraignment would be held and entered the courtroom where dozens of people were sitting, waiting for their turn to be arbitrated.

A few minutes past his time of arraignment, his name was called along with the case number. The assistant state attorney was a woman, a young woman, an attractive woman.

"Thank you," Mr. McMannus-Evans said. "My client, William Chute, has traveled here for this arraignment from Baltimore, Maryland, where he is an upstanding citizen. He comes from a long line of military servicemen; in fact, his father just recently returned from serving two deployments in Iraq. My client today is seeking a motion for nolle prosequi. As you will be able to see from the rather light discovery we have received, the charges cannot be proven due to the evidence being too weak to carry the burden of proof, as the evidence is fatally flawed in light of the claims brought. If you refer to page 6 of the discovery, you'll see—"

"—thank you Mr. McMannus-Evans," he was interrupted, "we will proceed with nolle prossed, contingent that the defendant enter a pre-trial diversion program in which he will be required to take 55 total hours of courses on drug use and complete 250 community service hours. If the defendant successfully completes the program within the next twelve months, Miami-Dade County will then drop all charges against the defendant. Does the defendant comply?"

Mr. McMannus-Evans looked at Billy with eyes that were encouraging him to say yes. Billy shrugged while nodding his head in confirmation.

"The defendant complies."

Down went the gavel and just like that, it was over.

✕ ✕ ✕

"Where you headed?" Mr. McMannus-Evans asked as they walked back toward his car.

"The fuck out of Miami, that's for sure. I'm going to keep on moving, you know?

"Where to?"

"Georgia." It just came out. But, in that moment, it felt right. To pick up from where he left off.

"Where can I drop you off?"

"The bus station will work."

"Well, I'm glad it's finally over for you," the lawyer said to him a few minutes from the bus stop. "Just so you know, we always move for expungement first, and if the judge will not grant it, we will ask for the records to be sealed. They both amount to the same thing. If granted, the files would be closed to all persons except if you are applying for a federal or state agency which would allow the opening of the file by statute in order to determine fitness for the license sought. For example, a nursing license will allow the opening of records relating to abuse, drugs, battery. Of course another arrest for a similar or like crime will allow access to the files. We will stay in touch with you throughout the process. And think about what kind of community service you'd want to do. You can do it anywhere in the United States with an appropriate agency. I'd recommend getting started earlier rather than later, and in small doses. About ten hours a week, and you'll be done in six months."

"I appreciate all you've done. You've really saved me."

"And I'm still getting the better of ya!"

"It's true—you wiped me out. Yet I think hiring you may have been the smartest thing I've ever done."

"We aim to please."

His lawyer finally said "safe travels" upon dropping him off, gave him a wink, and off he went in his Jag. Billy checked the Greyhound schedule and saw that the next available bus, which wasn't due to depart for another two hours, was indeed heading back up north—to Gainesville, Georgia with further stops through Cohutta National Forest along the Georgia-Tennessee border before making its way west to Chattanooga. *This'll work.*

Billy took a seat on a bench outside of the station close to his departure gate and opened his journal.

THE ESCAPIST

Fresh start.

He read back through his most recent entries and saw the sticky notes from a few days ago. He removed his collection of sticky notes from his bag, took off the rubber band, and flicked through them. He still had some time until the bus left, so he got up and went to the bookstore across the street from the terminal and glanced through some of the books and magazines on display. He stopped at a few science fiction titles and flipped through them. He browsed the fiction rack and found another book by Paul Auster, this time it was *The Book of Illusions*, read the first few pages and then decided to hold onto it while he continued perusing. He found *Heroes, Gods, and Monsters of the Greek Myths* by Bernard Evslin on the discount rack and while paging through it, came across the same three-headed dog from Gabriel's tattoo—Cerberus, he learned, guardian at the gates of the underworld. He sat down in one of the aisles, rested his back against the shelf, and continued reading about other immortal creatures and omnipotent gods.

He saw through the bookstore window that there was now a group of people that had lined up by his gate. With one of his few remaining crisp bills he paid for his books and then put the change back into his pocket. He had watched over the past couple of weeks his assets dwindle, his money, his pills, his pot, his edibles, his car, and it had been happening at a steady, and as of late, exponential rate, and spending just a bit more on some books suddenly felt only natural, like there was a sudden implicit goal in place to make it to $0.00, to hit rock bottom, to start again from scratch for yet another new beginning.

He got in line with the others. Billy took out his journal, stared at the cover of it for a short while, running his fingers over its many creases. Then he opened it and reacquainted himself with some of his earlier entries. The man standing behind him peered over Billy's shoulder and looked at the journal that Billy was focusing intently upon.

"Are you a writer?" the man asked.

"Huh?" Billy said without turning around.

"Sorry to bother you—I was just wondering—are you a writer?"

Billy didn't respond.

"What are you writing? If you don't mind my asking."

"This is nothing," he finally said as he closed the journal and turned around to look at the man. "Just some family stories and things." The man was a good fifteen years older than him, looking a bit haggard but muscular under a blue collared shirt that seemed one or two sizes too big, unshaven, dark bags, oily skin, saccadic eyes.

"So, then, you *are* a writer."

"Well, yea."

"That's great. I've always been envious of writers. If you can do it, I would say keep at it. It's an art form.

The greatest of art forms. Not to mention cheaper than therapy."

Billy nodded. He thought the guy may have been a little strung out from how he looked, but he wasn't really acting like it, wasn't shifting his body weight or doing any of the tweaks, and then Billy realized he was the one shifting around.

"I'm Bryan. Nice to meet you," he said.

"Daedalus," Billy responded back quickly, steadying himself, and it suddenly felt good to lie again, a thinned out defense mechanism.

"Daedalus. I see. Interesting name. Well, where you headed, Daedalus?"

"Oh, ah, going to Chattanooga, heading out to visit family. Was just here in Miami for vacation. But I'm from New York." He hesitated. "New York is where I lived, anyway. And you know what, I might just be heading back there. We'll see. Time will tell."

"Well, hey, I'm from New York, too. I grew up in Queens."

"I lived in Queens, too."

"Where abouts?"

"I lived in Astoria for a bit." He then realized he had just broken character, truth was seeping out, and he wanted to get back to playing Daedalus.

"Jackson Heights, myself," Bryan said. "Great to meet another Queens guy out here. Was just here for work. Construction. Yep, I'm making my way back home. I was going to fly, but I said to myself, what the heck! Let's do the God-lovin' Appalachian Trail! I'm gonna do the damn thing. Make my way as far as I can, anyway. I'll probably cut out at some point, find a town somewhere down the line, get a rental car and then head home to keep fighting the good fight—for the ninety-nine percent."

"The ninety-nine percent?" Billy asked, unaware of the growing Occupy Wall Street movement.

"Yes, sir. The ninety-nine percent."

"What's the ninety-nine percent?"

"It's the common man. The common man that is losing everything to the overlords of this country. I've got unfinished business with those fascists."

Billy didn't respond. He didn't know how. He had never cared much for politics, had never voted, never spent much time interrogating the political system he was born into. He nodded though, then he turned around to face forward again in line.

"Yep, I'm going to put in my two cents with the movement," Bryan said to the back of Billy's head. "Force them to see us. Force them to hear us. And they'll hear me alright. They'll finally hear me."

Billy turned his head and nodded again.

"But first things first," Bryan continued, "I'm getting off this bus at Springer Mountain, and then I'm off on foot, due north through Appalachia."

Billy turned back around. "How far does it go?"

"The Appalachian Trail? It's one of the longest hiking trails in the world. Maybe the longest. All the way up the eastern seaboard to Mount Katahdin in Maine."

"That's amazing."

"Yep. It's something I've always wanted to do. Something I always told myself I'd do before I die. I was contracted to work here in Miami for a year, but I left the job early. They need me in New York. But I told myself I had to do this first. Now or never."

Then the line started moving. Billy followed those before him onto the bus and took a window seat in the back. Bryan sat next to him without asking permission. After a few minutes, the bus powered on, the driver made a few safety announcements, and then they were on their way out of Miami. Billy opened his journal.

Finally leaving this godforsaken city. Finally back on the path. You're ready.

Billy then sensed he was being watched, and indeed, Bryan was looking on, reading the words Billy had just written.

"I couldn't have said it better myself," Bryan said. "I *am* ready."

Billy said nothing, caught off guard. Moments later, into the dead air between them, Bryan asked Billy if he had really never heard anything about the movement. Billy shook his head. Bryan then went on to explain about corruption in America as he saw it—big business tycoons running things in Washington, spreading wealth to their fellow hyper-rich and stripping the rest of the citizenry further and further down to nothing.

"It makes me sick. Sick to my stomach. Doesn't it make you sick?"

Billy nodded along.

"And you know why we've been in Iraq for the past eight years, don't you?"

"Yea. 9/11. Weapons of mass destruction."

"No. They threw us into this war in Iraq for the oil, to slurp up more money and power. You know who the only winners of this war are? Big Oil. And the cycle continues."

Billy thought just then that perhaps Bryan was one of those bleeding heart liberals Peter used to talk shit about.

"My brother was just there," Billy said, and as it came out he realized he had broken character again. "My father, too," he continued.

"They made it home ok?"

"They made it home ok."

"Thank God. And you, Daedalus? Did you serve?"

"No. It was pushed down my throat pretty hard," he said, still being honest. "I went to a boarding school which was basically like a feeder for the military. But I was never any good at fighting." He suddenly thought of his old roommate, Simi, and that last time he had seen him, decked out in uniform; he wondered if Simi had also been shipped off to Iraq, if he was even still alive. "What about you?"

"I've served my country," Bryan responded. "I will always serve my county. But no, I was not in Iraq. But this is what I'm talking about—your brother and your father were pawns in their grand scheme. They're part of this too. And you. If this was a true representative democracy, we never would have been in Iraq in the first place. All those lives would never have been lost. Your brother and your father never would have stepped foot into that country. This is a big part of that family story of yours. This is the kind of stuff you should be writing about."

Staring out his window, Billy did think about writing something down just then—that he was thankful for the war, thankful for those fascists, as Bryan called them, for sending his father away. But he put nothing down on the page. Instead, what was now puttering around in his thoughts was Bryan's strange curiosity and interest in him being a writer. And he liked the way it sounded. *Daedalus Chute, writer*. He pictured himself as such. As they continued to talk, Billy gave Bryan the impression that he was living a romanticized life, writing by candlelight, getting inspiration from walking the streets like Paul Auster's characters, listening to classical music, and having lots of sex against the ten-foot high windowpane of his apartment on 67th street where Central Park was his backyard.

Bryan told him that he loved Paul Auster, too. How much he loved Gabriel Garcia Marquez. About his love for Hemingway, Melville, Mishima. "And of course, Joyce. I'm sure you must love Joyce too, right Daedelus." Bryan added a small but noticeable emphasis to "Daedelus" when he said it, for the mythic name was the inspiration for James Joyce's protagonist, Stephen Dedalus, in *Portrait of an Artist as Young Man*, and when Bryan said it, Billy questioned if he was on to him. It was one of the few assigned books at Mission Mountain that Billy actually read all the way through. Bryan turned to what he was currently reading: Brinton's *Anatomy of Revolution* and Camus' *Rebel*, and Billy nodded along as if he had read them.

"So what kinds of family stories are you writing, Daedalus?"

His mind went back to Evslin's book. "The first book I wrote centered around the early years of Hades and Poseidon and Zeus and their sisters, when they were swallowed whole by their father, Cronus, but the one I am working on now is something closer to home."

"That is quite an achievement!"

Billy waved his hand modestly and told him that it was nothing. He suddenly felt so good to have this history for himself; he felt the dopamine flushing through. It instilled within him a noble sensation—he felt for a few short-lived moments the thrill and honor of being a writer—of being an artist.

"What do you do? You're a writer, too? An artist?"

"I am an artist, but a painter."

"Would I know any of your work?"

"Yes, you must…I painted *the Bordighera. Poplar Trees, Houses of Parliament*, pieces like that." Then he gave a quirky smile while his eyes continued to flutter. Bryan's response and the subsequent smile told Billy that he knew he had been lying about being a real writer, been lying about everything, and wanted to smear it in his face. Either that or Bryan was delusional and had an alter ego of the 19th century French impressionist painter, or like Billy, wanted to pretend that he was something he wasn't—to try gain the small fleeting pleasure of having a stranger believe in your greatness.

The bus was passing through the hills of Cohutta. Billy's journal was in his lap. His pack was right above them on the overhead rack, and Bryan was looking up at it through the metal bars.

"From the looks of it," he said, "it seems like you're not in such a rush to get back to the city."

"Not particularly, no."

"What do you say to joining me for a little hike? Springer ain't that bad of a climb."

Before Billy could answer, Bryan got out of his seat and walked through the aisle over to the driver. He talked to him for a minute and came back and sat down again with a smile on his face.

"There's another bus that'll be here in the morning. Same route and everything. You can use the tickets you've already purchased. You got boots?"

"Yea…"

"Come on, then!"

Billy didn't break from his expressionless forward stare and didn't respond. He still didn't quite know how to respond to Bryan. No one had ever taken an interest in him like this before, never so quickly.

After a short period of silence, Bryan turned his head and spoke softly to Billy again. "I think it would be in your interest to come with me. I've got a story, too. And I'm a man on a mission. My story will be told—that's a certainty. Perhaps you may want to be the man to tell it."

Billy stayed mute until the bus pulled into the Cohutta bus terminal, and it faced the world of Appalachia to its north.

"Well then, nice knowin' ya." Bryan sat for another few seconds waiting for some kind of response, some kind of acknowledgement of his being, but Billy didn't give it to him. He turned away and stood up along with a few others who were pulling down their bags and belongings from the overhead rack.

Billy watched as Bryan exited the bus. Bryan paused as he was walking away toward the base of the mountain which could be seen in the distance, and he looked back at Billy through the bus window. They briefly made eye contact, and then Bryan turned and kept walking. Billy stared forward again for a few more seconds, and as the bus driver was pulling the lever to close the bus door, he said "fuck it," abruptly grabbed his pack from overhead and grabbed Bubba. The bus had driven a few feet when Billy ran forward. The bus stopped again, the door opened, and Billy stepped off. When he was about to start chasing down his new friend, Billy looked up to see Bryan standing there in wait.

"You know, a little exercise will do me right."

"I'm glad you decided to come. It's going to be glorious at the top."

15

After changing into his boots, he followed Bryan to the trailhead. After only a few minutes of hiking, Billy was already imagining seeing his father somewhere deep in the brush. *Perhaps this is where you'll find him.* He had water bottles filled up from the fountain at the base of the trail and snack-mix in his bag that Bryan had given him before the start of the trek. There was another older gentlemen hiking up beside them who was also making his way up the mountain as well. He had hiking poles to help keep his balance.

"Do those poles really help?" Billy asked.

"Maybe slightly better than that walking stick of yours. They help me keep my balance. Good for the declines. An old man like me—I don't have the strength that I used to."

The three of them spent a lot of the hike up not speaking, but just having another person by his side made the hike go by faster. The physical exertion pacified the cravings, but he knew they were there, just behind him, also keeping good pace. He saw a deer, lizards, giant beetles. There was a light breeze, and as they got closer to the peak, every ten feet up, the temperature would drop by a degree or two. He kept a keen eye out for his father. He knew he wasn't going to be there, but he felt an inkling that he should have been there—that a place like this, out in nature, in the middle of nowhere, would be the perfect backdrop for a confrontation. He envisioned his father just popping out of the tree line and walking beside them to the top. He would be decked out in his fatigues with black face paint under his eye, guns clipped to his waist and ankle with a knife between his teeth. Billy then imagined a tarp on the side of the mountain with his father's rotting carcass. Pinned to his body would be a suicide note. Worms and bugs would be crawling through the crevices where his eyes used to be, one more recently than the other. Parts of his abdomen, legs, and neck pecked out by vultures.

It took three hours to reach the peak. A suspension footbridge took hikers from one peak to the next. At the highest point of the mountain, a rectangular shaped plaque read, "Appalachian Trail. Georgia to Maine. A footpath for those who seek fellowship with the wilderness. The Georgia Appalachian Trail Club." The plaque pictured a hiker with a rimmed hat, tall boots and a large shoulder bag, and what looked like a pickaxe attached to his waist. One of the eyes of the pictured man was hidden underneath the hat, as if nonexistent, but his other had a confident sideward glance, giving the man a look of fortitude, coolness—like he was paving the way for all of those that would follow.

Billy found it breathtaking at the top. He could see miles and miles of vast plush hills and open flatlands out to the horizon. To the north were over two thousand miles of Appalachian Mountains, appearing smaller and smaller in the distance, progressively more obscure with clouds and fog. The old man with hiking poles asked if Billy could take his picture with the mountains in the background.

Billy made his way to a rock on the side of the peak and took a seat. Bryan and the old man were on the other side of the peak, exploring different bends and crooks and the views they provided. Billy pretended he saw his father's tent in the distance. He saw himself walk up to him. He opened his journal and wrote out the first words that came to him:

Dad. It's me, Billy. I just wanted to say, go fuck yourself, you fucking asshole, you selfish piece of shit. Go jump off that fucking footbridge already. You're a crawling contradiction in everything you do. Go fall on barbed wire and choke on glass. Stick the knife in and twist. Pull your intestines out and then shove them down your throat and then back through your stomach and tie them in a knot and then wrap them around your neck and bind them to the railing at the top of that footbridge and jump you fucking horrible worthless insect. And if you're lucky, many years from now, out of your fertilized corpse flowers will grow, and those flowers will be the one and only positive thing you will ever contribute to this world. You'll at least bring a little beauty to this world once you take yourself out of it. Now go to that fucking bridge and do what I told you to do, you asshole. You don't know a goddamn thing about responsibility, do you? Your responsibility wasn't to them. Look what they did to you. They might as well have killed you. Your responsibility was to me. And I would have loved you. But look what you did to me. You used me. You fucking used me, you rapist. Now it's too late for you to take responsibility for me. Now, it's your responsibility to take yourself out. Listen to your conscience as it tells you to take yourself out of the equation. Listen to me, Dad, as I tell you to take yourself out of the equation. I am your conscience, and your life is not worth living. You have made me in your image, and I am a crawling contradiction just like you, you fucking asshole. I hate you. Now go do what you must. But first tell me that you love me. Tell me that you've always loved me and that you're sorry. Just say it. Just say it. Say it just once. Why can't you say it just once.

16

He felt under his eyes to see if there were any tears. They felt puffy, but there was no liquid. A series of heavy breezes were blowing through. Billy continued staring into the vastness in front of him. He opened his pack to the inside zippered compartment and rummaged through his drugs. He pawed at them, shuffled them around, picked up the pill bottles one by one, shaking them by his ear to hear how many rattled inside. He grabbed the psilocybin bag. Took it out and inspected it closely. He removed the three remaining caps and threw them in his mouth, chewed and swallowed them down with the little bit of water he had left. He dumped the remaining stems and final crumbs from the bag into his hand and ate that too. He licked his palm. Then he rolled up a joint and sparked it.

The old man with the hiking poles eventually walked past him, saw him smoking and said "enjoy it—you've earned it," and made his way down the mountain. Bryan resurfaced a few minutes later from the other side of the peak, walked over to Billy and scooted onto the rock next to him. He had his shirt off, and his skin was starting to burn from the sun.

"Are you working on something?" he asked, after seeing the open journal at Billy's feet.

"Kind of." Billy shut the notebook and slid it between his legs.

"I'm in awe of what you're doing. I really am. You should be proud of yourself, Daedalus." He put a hand on Billy's shoulder. Billy offered him the joint. Bryan took a small hit, inhaled sharply, and handed it back to him.

"I have a confession to make," he said as he exhaled the smoke. "I'm no real artist. When I saw you at the bus station with your head in your journal, well, it made me envious."

"Oh. Well, what do you do then?" Billy asked quietly, still staring out at the range in front of him.

"What do I do? I fight for things I believe in. The greater good. I want to make change in the world because there are things that I hate—things that I absolutely hate. I want to make real change, have an impact, I always have, and maybe that's why I wanted to be a painter in the first place, because painting has that power—art has that power. The things is, I've always loved painting, don't get me wrong, but, how can I put this…I'm terrible!"

Billy smiled.

"I still do it when there's some free time. I still like to get lost in the world I create with my paint. But after people see what I've created, they feel nothing from it. You know how I know? Because they tell me they like it."

"I don't get you."

"What I mean is, liking something isn't good enough. They need to love it. They need to be moved. And if they don't love my work, I would prefer they hate it— that they despise it. If I can cause that kind of rage in a person all with just some colored oils on canvas, that's a real feeling. And to be honest, even if someone said that they did love my work, that they just loved it, I don't think I'd get the same feeling, anyway. Love is a word people throw around too much. It's rare to hear someone use the word hate. For someone to truly hate. That's a special kind of feeling. Is there anything that you hate, Daedalus?"

Billy quickly cocked his head at Bryan, suddenly wondering if and how he was able to see any of what he had just written to his imaginary father.

"Yes, there are things I hate."

"I think that's good. I think a writer needs to have a certain amount of hatred. But me…I'm just a damn cliché to them. That's what I am. What my painting is to them."

"But as long as your paintings mean something to you, that's what's important right?"

"No, absolutely not. Shame on you for saying that. As a writer you should know better. It's *all* about the influence. The affect. That's what it's all about. As long as it means something to you—that's what you'd say to some failure. And thus my point, Daedalus. I'm no artist."

"Don't be so hard on yourself, man." Billy knew about being hard on yourself. "And I'm sure your paintings aren't half-bad."

"Half-bad? Half-good. Half-terrible. What does it mean for something to not be half-bad, anyway? It means not good enough. Forgettable. Meaning to blend right in with the crowd. And that's something I never wanted. I will not be forgotten. Trust me, you'll see."

Billy then remembered what Bryan had said on the bus, about him being a man on a mission, that his story would be told. That maybe Billy could be the one to tell it.

"So I don't waste my time painting any more," Bryan continued. "Now I preoccupy myself with other things, with real work, real causes. I've protested in so many damn rallies it's impossible to count. I've been jailed so many damn times. The construction work I was doing— just a means to an end."

Billy was looking at Bryan as he spoke, but his gaze quickly focused in on the footbridge behind him on the other side of the ridge, abruptly picturing his lifeless father dangling from it by his intestines. His focus returned to Bryan. "Well, what kind of construction work do you do?" Billy asked, though not really interested in the answer.

"Anything really. As long as I'm exerting myself. Pushing my body. Working hard. Sweating. That's what I do now. I sweat. I've gotten pretty good at fighting, too. Fighting for what I believe in. I've always been a fighter."

"For what?" The joint had gone out, but Billy was still holding it between his fingers.

"For what's right. For justice. But not the same justice as our legal system. Real justice. I believe that everyone should get a fair shake, no matter what. I've felt this way for a long time now. I'm just so fucking sick of all the prejudice. All the abuse. I love to see people that are willing to change the conversation. True revolutionaries. I guess it was this that made me want to become an officer back in New York, but that was a lifetime ago."

The comment threw Billy.

"Don't look at me like that."

"I'm sorry, I just, I don't like the police right now."

"That makes the two of us. It used to seem like the best job in the world until I realized that so many of them, from the very top, from the very top, Daedalus, are terribly corrupt. Bigoted assholes. Such disregard for the common man. For our humanity. They are stuck in a system and pedaling that system. They don't try to bend it and just keep on blending into it. A lot of them aren't bad. For a lot of them it's not their fault. But it's what got me out of it. What's your beef with the police?"

"I just got into a little trouble in Miami, that's all."

"Still in trouble?"

"Not really. I have some community service I need to do, some programs I have to attend."

"What did you do?"

"Murder."

"Murder?" Bryan looked alarmed.

"...no," Billy responded, shaking his head, gazing back at the footbridge in the distance.

"I see. Nothing too serious I hope."

"I don't really feel like talking about it right now, if that's ok." Just through broaching the subject matter, urges were swarming back into his brain, starting to pulse through his veins, and he thought he may need something stronger. He relit the joint and took a big puff, sucked the smoke in, and exhaled it through his nose.

"Daedalus, come with me."

"What do you mean?"

"I mean keep hiking with me. If you're not in a terrible rush, have some extra time on your hands. We can break whenever you need it. I have plenty of food for the two of us, up at least until the Byron Reese Trailhead where we can restock on food and supplies. There are towns along the way you know. There are places where you can stop. I don't know when I'm going to stop though. I might just keep going straight until I reach Occupy. I don't know yet. I'll get a sign. I always do. But it's pretty simple. We walk until we get hungry and then we eat. We eat until we're full and then we walk. We walk until we can't walk any more and we stop. We build a fire. We sleep when we're tired and swim when we're sweaty. I'm a quiet guy like you, so I won't bother you when you're writing. But you know, you have the freedom to do whatever you want to do."

Bryan started for the other side of the peak where the rest of his belongings were.

"What's the next closest town?" Billy yelled to him.

"Closest town is back where we started, Daedalus. But in about eight miles, we'll hit Hightower Gap where roads will lead back into civilization. You'll be able to get a shuttle back to the bus if you decide later to cut out."

Bryan kept walking and was soon out of view. The joint had gone out again. Billy tried to relight it, but the winds were too strong for the lighter to keep a flame. Billy gazed back over at the footbridge as his hair danced wildly in the wind. He saw his father hoisting himself up from the ledge of it with long octopus arms, then using them to dust himself off, then crossing them across his chest as he stared back at him. Billy turned away to the northern mountains. When he looked back again at the footbridge, he was gone. Billy slowly gathered up his things, tied his boots back on, picked up Bubba and lumbered over the rocky peak to Bryan. He walked past him with his eyes planted to the north, said "well, let's get going then," and started clumsily for where the trail continued.

"Drink this first," Bryan yelled and threw him a pint bottle of partly-drank water. "Drink the whole thing. Don't want you dying out here on me."

The hike down at first felt harder than the hike up. He fell into a groove with it soon enough, and then went his thoughts into the plains. The pain in his feet and legs dulled, but the hunger inside of his body and the famine inside of his brain continued to blaze.

Bryan tried less and less to chat with Billy because he saw that his words were going right through him, for Billy had fallen lost into his clouds. But these clouds were taking on a different form than with his other psilocybin trips. Less scattered. Mother Nature, it seemed to Billy, was helping induce this new iteration of the cloud. Having her all around him, breathing her into his nostrils, she was driving it. While his body continued down the mountain, his mind was elevating, rising, embracing the sun, looking down on himself and seeing his past selves, past directions, wrong directions, ones that would have otherwise seemed to have no causality, but they were all tethered together now and walking in procession like a slave gang. "It's all actually connected," he whispered through his teeth somewhere along the way. Bryan could see that Billy was having a moment and continued walking with his head down at the trail at his feet. Billy didn't realize he had spoken; his mind was too occupied, so occupied that halfway down the side of the mountain, he vanished—disappeared—and was now one with it, one with the man at his side, one with the world around him. This new pursuit was real and he was making it real.

They reached grassy foothills, and the hike stretched along a stream that speckled over onto the trail at times and it caused Bryan to do some leapfrogging from rock to rock so his boots wouldn't get wet. Billy's eyes were glossed over. The bottom half of his body was numb. He was stampeding right through the stream. Having soggy socks and squidgy feet didn't seem to bother him. They continued on for three and half more miles, Billy still in his inimitable daze, until they reached Hawk Mountain Shelter campground. Bryan and Billy cleaned up with the fresh running water, used the outhouse—just a hole in the ground with two wooden beams a few feet above it supporting a loosely-screwed plastic toilet seat, with clean toilet paper left by previous hikers perched upon the wooden beam but to Billy a gift from God due to the severe itch he felt in his behind now that his movement had stopped—and then Billy waited patiently for the next course of action for which he now felt the universe would direct him.

"We'll set up camp in the lean-to by that fire pit," Bryan said motioning toward a section that was about a hundred yards from the outhouse. The moon was getting brighter through the dark clouds above. Dusk was quickly becoming night.

Bryan built a small fire and boiled water for instant soup. They ate quietly, then Bryan lay down on top of his sleeping bag and read his book while Billy stayed sitting with his bare feet in the dirt over the side of the lean-to, smoking a cigarette with one hand and twisting Bubba into the earth with the other.

He threw his butt into the fire, then crawled to his sleeping bag. "What are you reading?" he asked.

"It's the first book length study on the act of self-immolation. Self-sacrifice. The age old tradition. Benn's *Burning for the Buddha*."

"Self-immolation?"

"Yup."

"Which is?"

"Setting yourself aflame."

"Sounds painful."

"Some say you pass out from smoke inhalation before the pain hits you. But screw it. I say, feel the pain. The strongest pain known to man. Death by fire. The truest test of strength. The noblest way to prove your worth, the way I see it. A real way to push a cause forward. Look at Bouazizi."

"Who?"

"Bouazizi. A simpleton working as a fruit vendor on the streets of Tunisia. The police were fucking with him and he stood up to it—set himself on fire in front of the government offices. It basically sparked the Arab Spring—got the whole Middle East to stand up and fight against the evils."

"Wow."

"Even a man with nothing holds tremendous power."

Bryan turned back to his book, but moments later, spoke again: "And speaking of, you know your name comes from Greek Mythology."

"I know."

"And you had some counterparts—Heracles and Dido. You know what they did?"

"What did they do?"

"They also committed self-immolation. Perhaps the first ones on record. Isn't that interesting, Daedalus? I knew it was a sign, right when I heard you say your name. I just felt it. Did you feel it too, Daedalus? Like a spark. A match catching fire."

Billy didn't respond. He may have felt it earlier, but now the drugs were just about worn off.

"Croesus, King of Lydia, what's now Turkey, did the same after losing to the Persians. Diocletian's palace was set on fire and then the Christians who started it threw themselves into it as a form of protest. Christians continued to do it—gathering in churches and setting them on fire in protest to changes to their religious traditions. The practice was made famous by those I'm reading about now—the Tibetan monks protesting China's rule."

Billy stayed silent. He lay on his sleeping bag and stared out at the stars and wondered how anyone was able to connect the dots and make out the constellations. To him they all seemed just like an infinite swirl of specs, existing in their own way, in their own solar system with no relationship, no invisible lines connecting them to any of the others.

Billy watched Bryan as he put his book down and as his eyes were starting to close. Within minutes, he seemed to be asleep, or in meditation, one of the two. Just beat from the hike, Billy considered. Billy stared at him for a while. There were a few other hikers around who had also set up camp relatively close by, and a few were staying inside the larger shelter. Billy opened his pack and reached for the pill bottle. He swallowed one of them, did a quick roll of the head. He gazed out toward the shadow of the mountains to the north. A generator attached to the shelter was humming in the background like a loud purring—a soothing meditative vigor.

He had to pee. He gave Bryan a tap and asked him if he had a flashlight. Bryan shifted around, rolled over and started breathing deeply again, a light snore. Billy crawled over to Bryan's bag and opened up a few of the different zippered pockets looking for the flashlight. In the big section were Bryan's clothes and another pair of shoes, more books, then packed into the bottom of the lower zippered section of the backpack he saw a twisted up plastic bag which contained a clear glass tube with a metal tip at the end of it, and Billy was suddenly looking at a needle and it looked back at him, confronted him, questioned him; the universe grabbed him by the shoulders and was now instructing him, testing him, leading him somewhere. The grand order of things was playing out right here in front of him and was happening because he wanted it to happen. *You wanted this to happen. A match catching fire.*

Billy held the needle through the plastic bag, shifted it around in his fingers, felt the weight of it, saw the yellow coloration caked onto the glass. His knuckles rubbed against the flashlight, and he remembered what he was looking for.

He slowly crawled back over to his sleeping bag and stared off into the stars. He pointed the flashlight to the sky and clicked it on and off, like an SOS to planes passing overhead. He remembered that he needed to pee.

After relieving himself, he burrowed back into his sleeping bag, removed his journal and his pen, rested the flashlight on the edge of the sleeping bag to light up the pages before him.

PART THREE

17

One year, and eight months. One year, and eight months since needle touched vein. You followed their regimen, took the methadone, did what they had you do at the clinic. Where Peter put you after he found you. He was back from Iraq, had survived the surge. Dad was still out there. But Peter wasn't finished rescuing. How the fuck did he know you were there. How the fuck did he know where to find you.

You were MIA from Mission Mountain. You and Stevo. You were so close to getting out of there for good, had already gotten through some of that first senior semester, but you just needed to get hooked up. And Stevo knew the place. He'd been there before. The two of you left school in the morning and walked to the station, took the train downtown. You followed him down this alleyway to the right of a building's loading dock. At the end of the alley was a small walkway, only about three feet wide. The walkway turned ninety degrees to the right leading to a squared off dirty area with loose pieces of cement.

That old disheveled teddy bear was there on the ground with

THE ESCAPIST

his feet sticking in the air. Stacks of wet newspapers were bunched together in a corner, maybe at one point someone's makeshift bed. Shards of glass, little bones with bits of old meat, wet and moldy clothes, a pair of shoes, all there on the ground, and then the dumpster in the other corner touching the wall of the feeble brown building. Above the dumpster was a cracked open window, covered by a white plastic tarp blowing in and out.

Stevo climbed on top of the dumpster and leaped into the window with little effort, appearing in that moment more dexterous than he really was. You swung your leg onto the dumpster, pulled your body up and lurched through the window after him.

Inside was a dark, empty, sooty room with tall blackened brick beams about ten feet apart from each other around the room. You didn't see Stevo. You walked through the room, then there was another tarp blocking a doorway. You pushed it aside and stepped into this next room, which looked more like a dungeon.

There was shuffling and movement. Suddenly, lots of faces. There was the man leaning against the wall with a big brown puffy beard and a dirty red hat, a big belly protruding out of a dirty white shirt. Next to him a skinny balding man with empty eyes, no shoes. Next to him an older man, stringy hair to his chin, eyes closed, uneven little snores. You walked past them. The first two were looking up at you.

Then someone grabbed your arm. It wasn't Stevo. It was this woman who was pretty filthy—long greasy hair running down her face like mud. Her grip on your arm was strong. She pulled you toward her corner, marked off with a hanging tapestry. She pointed to a baby lying there with a blanky over its body, thumb in its mouth. She held out her hand for something. For money, for help, don't know. Doesn't matter.

You just turned and walked away, kept going through the blackened hallways, then you spotted Stevo. He was sitting down against a wall next to a guy who was smiling with a hood over his head. The smile on the man's face wasn't a happy smile. His smile seemed stuck in a locked position. His eyes held all of the sadness that his mouth lacked. Sitting next to them was a lady in a short blue dress. She was sitting with her knees folded to the side of her. She held a handkerchief, was grasping it tightly. Her hand and arm shook from the force of her grip. Then the needle went in. Then her whole body eased.

You sat down next to Stevo, not giving one fuck about any of those people you saw. Stevo was already prepped, his arm wrapped, and then the smiler lit him up.

Then it was your turn. Then that's where you stayed. And stayed you did for a good long time. How long? Who knows. Doesn't matter. But that's where Peter found you is what he said as he was sitting there next to you inside the clinic with the iv drip in your clean arm. You didn't ask him how he found you. Maybe Stevo tracked him down and told him where you were. Maybe he called you and you answered in your oblivion and told him. Maybe you called him. But you won't ask him. Cause it doesn't matter.

The methadone did its job. You stopped with the needles. You finished school. But the void remained. And you used everything you could find to fill it.

THE ESCAPIST

Billy awoke, still burrowed inside of his sleeping bag, his face down on top of his journal. Drool had smudged some of the words he had written the night before, words he had written into the early morning. His forehead was moist with sweat, and his genitals and legs were damp with the stale residue. Billy flipped the sleeping bag off of his body, and the sun's beams were strong. Billy looked around the lean-to and saw that he was alone. There was no trace of Bryan, Bryan's backpack nor any of his stuff. His flashlight remained, and it was resting at Billy's side in the middle of the lean-to, still on and illuminating the wood paneling in front of it. He picked it up and clicked it off, stood, stretched, took out a change of clothes from his bag and walked down to the water to wash himself off and change. He felt dizzy, but the cold water equalized him. The sun was bright, and Billy thought that it must have been pretty late into the day already. He got back to the lean-to, rolled up and tied his sleeping bag, threw the pack onto his back, picked up Bubba, and walked around the Hawk Mountain Shelter campground looking for his partner. The other people that had set up camp in the area had already gone too, tents packed up, fire pits doused with water. Billy walked to the shelter with the humming generator and knocked on the door.

"Enter!"

He pushed the door open. Inside were bearded men sitting at a table upon which were paper plates with caked-on beans and rice leftovers, empty cartons of instant noodle soup at their feet. Cards were being dealt.

"Well good day to you, sir!"

"Hello. How's it going?"

"Just fine here my friend. You a thru-hiker?"

"A thru-hiker?"

"Yea, you going thru?"

"Going through what?"

"Oh boy. We got a newbie here."

"I'm sorry, I'm just looking for someone."

"We're all looking for someone, aren't we?"

"Well, I guess so."

"I'm Swamp-ass, and my fellows here are Genghis Khan and Finger Monkey."

"Oh, okay…"

"You doing a day hike? You here with your parents or something? Is that who you're looking for?"

"What? No." Billy shifted his weight from foot to foot.

"Then where you hiking to, fellah?"

"I don't know exactly."

"Definitely not a thru-hiker," Finger Monkey said quietly without looking up from his cards.

"What do you mean by that?"

Finger Monkey didn't respond. None of them spoke, but Billy stood there, still shifting his weight, and continued to stare.

"So look," Swamp-ass finally said as he threw a card down on the table. "A thru-hiker is someone who hikes through the A.T. from start to finish, Georgia to Maine, NOBO. Northbound. Hence, a *thru-hiker*."

"Then by all means, I could be that, sure."

"When did you decide that?"

"Well, I don't know. Just right now, I guess, talking to you."

"Okay…You got a trail name yet?"

"A trail name? Like, what kind of trail name?"

"Wow. Well. Your name is Newb then, as far as I'm concerned. Until you're ready for your real trail name."

"My name's Daedalus."

"Now you're cooking, Newb. That's thinking on your feet."

"No, that really is my name."

"And I'm really Swamp-ass. And as I said, this is Genghis Khan and Finger Monkey. Pleased to make your acquaintance. So who are you looking for?"

"I'm looking for a friend I hiked in with. His name's Bryan."

"Not sure. What did he look like?"

"Kinda tall guy, thirties, maybe forties, something like that. He's got a beard. Not like you guys got beards. Less growth to it."

"I think he's talking about Johnny Rocket," Genghis Khan chimed in. "Yea, that's gotta be Johnny Rocket. Cargo shorts? Brown pack?"

"Yea, that could be him. Why'd you call him Johnny Rocket?"

"Cause he just jet-packed the hell on out of here. I saw him take off this morning. He was hustling fast, stormed out of here like a rocket."

"I was supposed to be hiking with him."

"I guess not."

Billy rubbed his forehead with his fingers.

"I guess you're unaware of the dark magic of the Appalachian," said Finger Monkey. "He might just be gone. To pave his own path. People come here to start anew, after all. To forget the old. That's what these trails do to you. Maybe the magic had already gotten to him. If he needed to go, than that's what was necessary, maybe not just for him, but for you too, Newb Daedalus."

"But he's my friend. He was the one that got me here in the first place."

"I doubt that, Newb Daedalus. You're here because you got yourself here. What, did he drag you by your hair all the way from the trailhead?"

"No," Billy pondered. "But I have something that belongs to him. And I have his flashlight. He's definitely going to need his flashlight."

"You don't need anything out here on the trail. Just a clear head and facial hair. Johnny Rocket's already got his beard."

"I guess."

"Well," said Swamp-ass after another silence, "good luck out there on the trail." Then Swamp-ass turned his attention back to their card game, ending the conversation. Billy stood there not knowing what else to say and watched Finger Monkey as he shuffled then dealt the cards out. They were done with him.

"Thanks," Billy said.

"See you on the trail, Newb Daedalus," Finger Monkey said without looking up.

Billy shut the door to the shelter, did a 360 degree turn surveying the campground, noticed, then fixated upon a white streak of paint on a rock at the head of the trail that led out of the campsite and then farther north. Twenty feet in front of it was another white marker, this time on a tree, and then another twenty feet or so in front was a third white marker on another tree on the right side of the trail instead of the left. They told newbies what to do, where to go, to not ask questions and just follow the road of white dashes on out of that campsite—to follow the path that had been blazed already. The feeling and the sound of nature, the initiative—it washed over him then and there and then stayed. He was feeling the souls of the hikers that had traveled before him, the ones that paved the trail, and the soul of that first thru-hiker pictured on the plaque at the top of Springer Mountain, and they were whispering through the trees and were guiding him toward his inevitable end. These others that had sculpted this path he was walking were designing, too, he decided, the grand scheme of his life to come. All the work had already been done and laid out before him. He simply had to follow what they were asking of him. They were guiding him in the direction of forward without giving a reason, and Billy didn't have to ask them why. He accepted the world that they had marked, flagged, cairned and carved for him. He had already fallen into the design, he realized. Bryan's disappearance was a sign. It fit into his sequence as it was supposed to, his yearning for those that had been a part of his life but subsequently left him, and didn't want him to find them.

He stared down at the earth at his feet, at his boots taking one step and then the next, at Bubba as it punched the soil on the same beat as his feet. Before long, it turned into a rhythmic cadence, in line with his pulse; within minutes, he fell into himself once again. As he walked, a dragging protracted mantra ricocheted around in his mouth, in his headpiece, brought on by something Swamp-ass had said. *"Your parents—is that who you're looking for?" Your parents… your…mommy.*

She too was lost to him, the first to have left, but he knew of a place where she could be found.

The one thing you'll never forget. Mom's letter. Even if you end up old and wrinkled and lost like Grandma, her words will still be there. You've read it so many damn times, practically learned how to read because of it. It might as well be tattooed on your chest:

--Writing is a funny thing for me. I have all these thoughts and

feelings stored in my head, so much of it gets confusing and overwhelming, and I can't imagine how they will take form here, but as I sit with pen to paper, all I can think about is you. You are the reason I do what I do now. I wake to the thought of you and fall asleep to the thought of you. Five places I have lived in my life, fell in and out of love time and time again, did my time in school, three different jobs, four different states, a trip to Europe, one cross-country journey, bouts with inner-demons, lots of losses and a few wins, friend's weddings, multiple seasons of strange weather, laughter and tears, tears and laughter, and very soon, the welcoming of a new love, and that is you, my love. And this is a love I will never fall out of. You are mine and will forever be mine, and I, I will forever be yours. My love for you continues to grow, morphs and multiplies, even though I haven't even met you yet. I love the thought of you and everything you will grow up to become. Now and forever. I see you as if you were already here, right beside me, and I love having you here, and I love just looking at you. No matter what happens, no matter how hard life can get, just remember that I will always be thinking of you and will never ever let you go, no matter what happens to me and no matter what direction life takes us. You will one day grow up to find out that life is never what it seems to be. It will get hard, so hard sometimes that you'll want to cry, even if you can't. Life has been hard on me, and I've shed many tears. But right now I'm just so happy because I have you. And when it feels like life is getting too hard for you, just try to remember that one day you'll be happy like this, too. But until that time comes, just know that ~~your dad and~~ I will always be there to wipe away your tears, and if there are no tears, then I will be there in wait, patiently and proudly, until the tears come, and then I'll comfort you for as long as you need it and will hold you for as long as you need holding. And if God does decide to take me too soon, I will remain above, looking down upon you always, and all you'll have to do is think of me and know that I'm with you. Forever yours, my sweet.

18

It was a different kind of feeling to write her words. He had never done it before. It made him feel like he was touching her, and it gave her words new meaning. He felt like she was inside him as he wrote it, like he had been for her.

And he felt her as he walked. He kept at a breezy pace yet still had to stop periodically to build back up his strength, catch his breath, eat some of his trail mix that Bryan had given him back at Springer. After leaving Hawk Mountain Shelter campground, he passed through Hightower Gap, across Gooch Mountain, through its shelter and campground and after searching for his partner and not finding him, he continued across the Gooch Mountain Gap to Woody Gap and finally to Big Cedar Mountain where his body collapsed for the evening.

He slept the night in the corner stock bed of a shelter room which some other hikers were using too.

He didn't have the energy to make conversation; he was too exhausted, both physically and mentally. The other campers had made a stew concoction of beans and hot dogs and offered some to Billy. Without saying thanks he accepted their offer and ended up eating three bowls. He hadn't realized how hungry he was. Once the food started going down his throat, he couldn't stop. When Billy woke up, they were gone, but he found more bags of trail mix, leftover beans and hot dog stew, and four plastic bottles of water sitting at his side. *Trail magic.*

He ate the stew and packed the rest of the supplies into his bag and continued walking, following the markers to his next destination. He crossed Henry Gap, Jarrard Gap, Woods Hole Shelter campground, Bird Gap and walked part of the Freeman Trail which led to Slaughter Creek, where he submerged his head into the water and lapped the water up with his tongue.

Then he saw the sign for Blood Mountain—a nine mile incline. It was the tallest peak in Georgia and a crucial point for many Appalachian Trail hikers, Bryan had told Billy. It was the time when many hikers considered the trail to be too much, too brutal to endure for another two plus months. Billy approached the Herbert Reese Trailhead, and there were many day-hikers at the base. He could tell by their small bags, and by their ages. Either too old or too young to do this for any extended period of time. Others were starting their Appalachian voyage here. They had the big packs and the right gear, but clean hair, shaven faces or well-manicured beards. Then there were the others who were calling it quits. These were the ones that looked a lot like Billy. The dirty ones with ghostly complexions, ones with bad gear. But Billy pushed on. Other hikers were in front of him, in back of him, passing him, all along the trail now. It was getting congested with traffic. They were walking in the same direction as Billy, in the direction the markers were pointing, but there were a few that diverted from the path, walked the opposite way, like swimming upstream, and it was an odd sight to see for Billy. He felt that they were going against the natural order of things.

The trail evened out to flat terrain where the Walasi-Yi Mountain Center was located. It was the only walk-through building of the whole Appalachian Trail. It was built over the trail itself and to continue on, one had to walk through the doors of the building. It functioned as a gift shop and supply center. Billy felt the hunger stewing inside of him as he looked at the dry food that was available for sale. He quickly collected a handful of beef jerky and bags of nuts and dried fruits and brought them to the counter. He saw a few postcards for sale, which had pictures of the top of Blood Mountain, and decided to buy a few.

He walked through the building to the other side and continued on the trail as it hugged the corners of the mountain and zigzagged up to a rock garden. It was a large patch of land that had natural rock formations throughout, rocks balancing on top of other rocks, oddly shaped boulders with mismatched colors, some sticking out of the ground like diamonds. *The artistry of God.*

Billy walked through the garden, where many families were scattered about. Pictures were being taken, and families were posing. Mothers and fathers with children. Holding hands. Laughing and loving. Shining and happy. He pictured himself as one of these bright young faces who had the perfect life with the perfect mother and the perfect father. A mother that had not been lost so long ago and a father that was there to protect him from the thorny bushes on the trail and the sharp edges of the rocks that came too close to his head. The mothers and the fathers were together, with one another, too. They held hands, they protected each other. And their lives weren't dictated by psychoactive substances.

As Billy sat in the rock garden, he reached into his bag and took out one of the pill bottles. His lip flinched, and he rolled his head. He shook the pill bottle and heard that only a few remained, then he shook the others one by one and they too were running low, some already empty, and the nearsighted notion was suddenly quite calming: being one step closer to nothingness. Finally embodying a zero sum, becoming the mathematical empty set—that perplexing axiom in set theory pushed on him by Mr. Harris at Mission Mountain, who had been right in his sense to push, as he knew he could reach into Billy with it. The pills were assets, possessions, and he felt then that they also needed to be done away with, as no immutable substance exists in nirvana. *For all your bare elements to scatter like ash across these mountains.*

At the top, Blood Mountain had panoramic views—mountains and sloping hills in every which direction, and in the far distance, Billy could just make out the Atlanta skyline. He pondered if his father could be somewhere within that metropolis, in one of those distant high-rises, or perhaps roaming those city streets, or perhaps dead and decomposing behind some alleyway dumpster. He sat and stared for a while, at the distant hills, but also at the others that came here to have their breath taken from their lungs. He was able to identify the thru-hikers from the day-trippers. The thru-hikers all wore badges to distinguish themselves. It was their beards, their clothes, their packs, their odors, their dirt. These were the ones also following the signs, the white dashes, and Billy felt a sense of belonging with them. Some were doing it in groups; more were doing it alone. The day-trippers seemed suspicious of Billy, and he noticed that they were acting suspicious of some of the others, too, that were going thru. They were society's outcasts, hobos. Billy learned that a girl had been kidnapped and killed here at Blood Mountain a few years ago by a wandering derelict.

Billy noticed parents were keeping their children at a distance from him. So he picked up his things and moved on. He reached Wolf Laurel Top, which had a campsite and a view of foggy brown mountain tops at a clearing to the right. He was still keeping an eye out for Bryan, but again, his partner was nowhere to be found.

The next day, Billy continued through Tesnatee Gap, to Whitley Gap, Hogpen Gap and the Low Gap Shelter campground, which had a cove with a spring and stream a few hundred feet from the trail. He washed off, and drank till he was full. There, on a tree next to the stream was another marker, though this one was orange and it caught Billy off guard. The orange markers continued along the stream, offering another route for those looking to get off the beaten trail. He nodded. It ran parallel to the trail he had been walking and was beckoning him. So he took it.

It led him to Chattahoochee Gap. The world was quiet around him. It felt to him now like he was the only person in the world. He reached a tributary that led into the Chattahoochee River. He disrobed, sank his naked body fully into the water. He swam in circles, then the dead man's float.

Rain started to fall. A cloud had rolled in within only a couple of minutes. It drizzled on him, and he swam back to the edge of the river and shook himself off. Still naked, he threw on his boots without tying them, picked up his clothes and his pack, and walked quickly to Rocky Knob shelter campground, which was close, back at the head of the trail. It was all empty lean-tos, and he got under the closest one.

The rain began to pour—he thought of them as bullets shooting down from the sky—creating more fog. The lean-to had holes in the roof, but he was able to find a dry space to lay out his sleeping bag. He reached for dry clothes in his bag, but then he thought better of it. He wanted to remain naked, for he was aroused now and was touching himself. He watched his hand stroking his genitals. Then he closed his eyes and pretended it was Bernice's hand that was touching him, but the fantasy dimmed quickly because it never happened, so he couldn't quite conjure it; then it was him again, alone in the wilderness. But now it was Nicole's hand, her face close to his, her warm breath on his neck, then it was Melanie Rae's breath on his neck, her indulgent pubescent moaning in his ear, but the breath on his neck reeked just then, of that musky sweetish-sour he would smell on his father late at night, and it was his snorting and the glow-in-the-dark ceiling stars above him in his bed, and then just the ceiling stars.

Sometimes it even seemed like those ceiling stars were twinkling.

It continued raining bullets throughout the night. The rain stopped briefly the next morning before quickly picking up again. Staring out into the rain, Billy counted on his fingers how many days he'd been in Appalachia. It was now day seven, he realized, since waking up alone at Hawk Mountain Shelter campground.

He had put his plastic water bottles outside the lean-to to collect rainwater—like the mountains knew that he was running out of water so they decided to give him something to drink, like they knew that he needed a respite from his journey so they gave him time to recover. The mountains also knew that he didn't have food left. The pills would suppress his appetite, but not for long, for it was here on the trail that his supply would finally reach its depletion. Billy nodded along to them and gave thanks as his last two pills slid down his throat. He was buzzing before long with the wet world outside of his lean-to, and the sense of wellbeing returned—the last stretch to zero, to nothingness; it was in sight.

Billy's mother was still with him, there in the lean-to, he felt. He tried to imagine what Corinth would have looked liked if she were still alive. When someone dies, they stay the same age forever for all those that had known them, and he knew she was beautiful from the pictures, and he knew she'd still be beautiful today. He remembered how his grandmother would always say how much he looked like her when he was young. Then he tried to imagine what he would look like as an older man, and the portrait appeared to him as a warped version of his father, a being created by a mad doctor who performed the art of cloning, and he suddenly felt like that older man he was picturing as his body continued to hum, his dopamine receptors singing. He opened his journal.

That mad doctor, making incongruous clones, one after the other, in an endless loop of recycled organic matter, of stardust, so time is merely a mirage. A hole with nothing in it, the enduring zero, the empty set. And that loop is in you, in everyone, and it manifests. Manifests in grandma, her mind on loop as she proceeds closer to zero. Everyone on repeat and not even knowing it, or knowing but pretending it's not there inside of them. Somewhere in the back of their minds they know it's all they are, but they're all running from it, finding ways to ignore it, escape from it.

He wanted his dopamine receptors to sing louder, just then. He wanted them to scream. He reached for his bag. But there was nothing left of what had been his huge stash.

He got out from his sleeping bag, still naked, and reached his hand outside the lean-to to feel the rain. Then he stepped out into it and let it run through his hair, down his head, and all down his body. He raised his face to the sky with his eyes closed, and he just stayed like that as the mad doctor rained down on him.

When he was back under cover, he wiped himself

down with his shirt, then got back into his sleeping bag. He opened back up his journal.

When he woke early the following morning, the world was still wet, but the sun was breaking through the low-hanging clouds, and it was suddenly bright. It was one of those rare sun-showery moments—Appalachia produced them, even striking double arcs of rainbows from one valley to another—and one had appeared right in front of his eyes. The colors were wild, unnatural even in their morning brightness.

It wouldn't be long until the trail would be completely dry. His stomach was growling. It was now his second day without food and the drugs were gone, but that one escape was still lingering. The plastic bag and its contents that he had found in Bryan's pack, now reallocated to the bottom of Billy's pack, from one zippered pocket to the other that night at Hawk Mountain—and now he was holding it, clutching it tightly, now flashing back to the very first time he held this hydrochloride salt in his hands, to the playground with the merry-go-round a few blocks from Mission Mountain. The red, orange, yellow, green, blue, indigo, and violet glistened in front of his eyes. Billy took out the sticky notes from his bag and drew out the chemical honeycomb.

19

The long-faced father with octopus arms came to you in your dreams.

These were Billy's words, a product of his own manufacturing, yet it was what Alan had become. The image was more a reality than the man himself, and it coalesced into being in this dream he was living, his sweetest escape, creeping out from behind some distant rock.

He was now in his bed back in Baltimore, back in time, but a kid again, on a cool summer morning, and he was alone, and happy to be alone, his father and brother deployed, and he was now staring down upon the blank yellow square of a sticky note. He drew a picture of an octopus man on the sticky note then crumpled it up and threw it away, and that was its genesis, but just as quickly forgotten. The image hadn't returned until in a journal entry while half asleep in his car on the side of the road in Miami. And now, as Billy was lying upon the moist surface of the earth with a motionless hand bearing a pen and a soiled journal to his side, a needle sticking out of his arm, somewhere lost in Appalachian nothingness, beard on his face, red swollen watery eyes with miotic pupils, tattered clothing covering his decrepit body, with all other thoughts finally dulled to a stillness, the image had reappeared, and it had taken on new life.

It had come again through his fingertips upon the canvas of his journal like a divine proscription, out of his control. The words he imagined analogous to truth, his body just the conduit, and this was where he could find his father.

It was like Alan was there now, whispering to him through the trees, conveying to Billy that life was a fascinating dream with such mythological creatures, that he was one of them, that Billy could be the same, that Billy could be whatever he wanted to be, that he was indeed a special boy with a special mind.

Something made Billy's incubated eyes swagger out from his skull, and he felt his body being rolled over as the physicality of the world returned. "Come back to me," he heard a familiar voice saying. "Snap back," the voice said. "Snap out of it, wake up, c'mon now, that's it." His blurred vision came into focus and his eyes coasted to the diaphanous half-moon in the blue sky above.

Billy glanced to his side, and Bryan's face was looking down at him. The slightest smile crept across Billy's face. "We did it," Billy whispered back through his cracked lips, but as his smile reached its crest, *sleep* he heard summoned in the low drawl of another's voice and his eyes closed again. *Sleep*. Billy let out the soft hiss of the *s,* and then mouthed the rest of the word as his eyes shut again. It was the long-faced father with octopus arms who was appearing to him and telling him to sleep. Back from the dead, back from the cosmos of the world's unconscious. The long-faced father with octopus arms rose, taking his proper shape and growing solid, springing into being from the words written by his son. *And the long-faced father with octopus arms will live.*

PART FOUR

20

Billy opened his eyes. White squares of stucco ceiling. And there was his body, resting in a bed, legs under a blanket. In some room. Had he been here for days, weeks? He couldn't be sure.

"Good morning."

Bryan was sitting there next to him.

"Where am I?"

"You don't remember?"

"No…how did I get here?"

"You don't remember anything?"

"I don't know," Billy said, looking back up at the stucco. "Just being in the mountains. Walking. And walking and walking and walking."

"That's it? What's the very last thing you remember?"

Billy thought for a moment. "Swimming. Rain. A rainbow." Billy then saw his journal sitting on the corner table close to Bryan, and it was immediately clear to him that Bryan had had his hands all over it.

THE ESCAPIST

"Daedalus." Bryan shifted his eyes under his eyelids, then opened them again. "Billy. I never should have left you alone. That morning at Hawk Mountain, when I saw my bag open. When I saw you found my shit. I panicked. I ran. I should have known better, Billy. I should have been smarter. I should've thought about what I was doing. Leaving a kid like you with that. I was being selfish. The first thing I thought about was myself, about how it could incriminate me again. How it could put my whole mission in jeopardy. I got back on the trail and headed as fast as I could for the main road out of there. Wanted to just get as far away as possible. I didn't want to get into any more shit than I was already in. But I changed my mind. I missed you, Billy. We had this real connection. And I wrecked it. I knew I needed to go back and find you. Because I think I need you, and I will need you, and I think you need me too. And it's a good thing I did go back. You were practically dead by the time I found you."

Billy remained motionless, looking at Bryan intently and hanging off each word.

"I had gone back to the campsite at Hawk Mountain later that first day and you had already left. I found those guys in the shelter—what were their names? Finger Monkey? Swamp-ass? They told me you had moved on, kept on with the hike. So I did the same thing. I asked just about everyone I saw about your whereabouts, anybody who could have seen you. A few were able to point me in the right direction. The longer it took me to find you, the more upset I got. It was just by chance that I decided to take the back route behind the main path at Low Gap, and when I got to Rocky Knob, that was when I saw you. Face down in the mud. I thought for sure you were dead."

"Wait, wait. Where am I?" Billy tried to sit up.

"You're in my apartment. We're in New York. Billy, you don't even know what I had to go through to get you back here. You really don't remember anything? Do you realize what I'm telling you? You could be dead right now. Or, if someone else happened to find you, you'd be in some hospital with cuffs around your wrists. You understand what I'm telling you?"

Billy looked away in the other direction and out the bedroom window.

"Granted it was my fault," Bryan continued. "It was mine before you stole it from me, but the police never would have known. They just would have arrested you for possession and thrown you right back into lockdown. You must have taken a shitload of that heroin, Billy. I mean, shoot, were you trying to kill yourself? Lucky I had an ampule of naloxone on me."

"You had narcan on you?" Billy said, turning his gaze from the window.

"Of course…Because I dope the right way. I'm careful."

Billy winced at Bryan and then turned back to the window.

"Fell back into it in Miami. It had been eight months," Bryan said into the silence.

Out the window Billy watched the familiar array of taxis and trucks speeding by, the throng of pedestrians, listened to the cacophony of the city. "One year, eight months," he responded. "But I was never clean. Might as well have been no time at all."

"I'm done, myself," Bryan said. "I need to be now."

Billy tried to sit up again. "Give me my journal."

"Yea, yea, sure."

Bryan handed it over to him. Billy placed it to his chest.

"How the hell did I end up back in New York City?"

"After I found you, saw you were still breathing, I squirted the naloxone up your nose. Stayed with you at Rocky Knob another night. Got some water down your throat. You kept snapping in and out of sleep."

Billy then remembered seeing Bryan's face staring down at him, moving muted lips.

"I was too," he continued. "I kept waking up all night. Weird though—I remember, a few times in the night, you were writing again, like sleepwalking...sleepwriting. It was some of the weirdest shit I've ever seen. You'd write something down then fall back asleep. Finally, probably at like 2 or 3 in the morning, you were sleeping pretty good, not stirring, and I knew I couldn't just sit there. I ran down the trail, in the pitch black, and I'm talking *ran*, got to town, got a rental. Drove it back up through the access roads until I was close to Rocky Knob. Did a little off-roading up to the site. You were still out. I carried you to the car and drove you all the way back to New York. I only stopped once besides for gas, and that was to sleep for an hour. I still have to clean the vomit out from the car."

Billy was staring back out the window. He didn't react to what Bryan was saying, but being belted down to the backseat of a car was now registering. Being hoisted out of the car, lugged into the building and then plopped down into bed was now coming back in too. He brought his stare forward to his legs again and then shut his eyes. "You did all that for me?"

"Of course."

"It's a miracle you found me."

"We found each other, Billy." Bryan looked at the journal on Billy's chest. Touched it. "Actually Billy, that's not all. I'm sorry, but I read your journal. Some of it anyway. Curious if I was in there at all. If you had started writing about me yet, about us. But there's some sad stuff in there about your father. And about your brother."

"My brother."

"Yes, your brother, Peter."

"I called him," he said after a pause.

"You called my brother? Why the fuck would you call him."

"I don't know. For you. I called him, for you. I was

scared for you, I guess. I got your cell phone and found his number."

"What did you tell him."

"I told him, Billy, I told him that you had made a mistake."

"What kind of mistake."

"I told him that you accidentally took some drugs."

"Did you tell him what kind of drugs?"

"He knew, Billy. I didn't have to tell him."

"Of course he did."

"When he asked where I was taking you, I told him I was taking you back to New York, that that was where you were heading. I told him I'd take care of you. Then he asked me if you had been able to find your father. I told him I didn't know. He said you'd been looking for him. He wondered if what you did had anything to do with that. Does it have anything to do with that, Billy?"

Billy remained silent but rubbed his forehead with his palms.

"He wanted to know how you found out."

"How I found out what?"

"How you found out. You know. You know? How you found out—look Billy, look, let's just try getting a little more sleep," Bryan said as he stood up. "I gotta get some sleep, anyway. That's for sure. You should too."

Bryan stood up, walked for the door, then turned back around. "I know you're not gonna be hungry, but try to eat at some point. You need to eat. Just force it down. There's yogurts and snacks and things in that mini-fridge on the floor by the closet."

Bryan walked back over to Billy, grabbed his hand, kissed it. Billy didn't move. Bryan walked out of the room, closed the bedroom door. Billy heard it lock behind him. Billy turned back to the window. Once the crying started, it wouldn't stop.

✕ ✕ ✕

When the crying finally did stop, he picked up his journal and read. He got out of the bed but didn't realize how weak he would be. His legs were shaking. He shuffled his feet over to the door and jiggled the handle even though he knew he was locked in. He shuffled over to the side of the bed and sat in the chair. Read through more of his journal. It was almost all filled up with his words. He stood back up and opened the mini-fridge and found bottles of water, the yogurts, fruit cups. He tried drinking some of the water, but it was hard to keep it down. Every swallow brought on the nausea.

After nightfall, Bryan still had not returned to the room. Billy tried to hear for any stirrings outside of the bedroom door but couldn't tell for sure if Bryan was there. He wasn't able to sleep. In the dark, it looked like there was a figure in the shadows sitting in the chair at his bedside, and Billy imagined his mother sitting there, humming to him a lullaby, and he was, just for an instant, a baby again, safe at home.

21

Billy woke still disoriented. He looked around this mysterious room, and it took a few seconds for him to remember where he was. The memory from yesterday's events registered for him, and he fell back into himself. He looked behind him and saw that the bedroom door was open. He swung his feet out of the bed, and when he placed them on the floor and put his weight upon them, a tingling sensation ran up his legs as the blood made its way down. Starving suddenly, he went to the mini-fridge, took out a yogurt and sucked it down, gagged. He walked into the kitchen. Bryan was drinking a cup of coffee and looking through a newspaper with a pen in hand.

"How did you sleep?"

"Not so good." Billy stuck his mouth under the kitchen faucet and took some heaving gulps.

"It'll start getting better. Well, it'll get worse, then it'll start getting better. You gotta just give it time."

"How do you know so much about this," Billy asked as he joined Bryan at the small kitchen table.

"I've had a lot of practice. Like you, I guess. Just on the other side of it in the beginning." He took another sip of his coffee. "It's why I lost my job. With the NYPD." He wiggled the pen between his fingers. "This real asshole of a guy, Carabasa, he was my partner for a short time—he found out I was using and then snitched on me, I'm sure of it. The department did a drug test, they said it was random, but I knew they were hankering to find a way to get rid of me. When the test came back, I was booted out of there so fast I didn't even have time to clean up my desk."

Billy scratched at his ear. "Hey, you got a cigarette?"

"I got yours." Bryan walked to the adjoining living room where he had slept the night before—apparent from the pillow and splayed blanket on the couch—then walked back to the kitchen and threw the pack on the table. He poured the last of his coffee from his mug into the sink and put a splash of water in it, then set it in front of Billy to use for ashing. He took a lighter out of the drawer and placed it onto the pack.

"Yep, I knew all about it before I started," Bryan continued. "I used to find people all smacked out when I was on my beat. I carried an atomizer for that very reason. With any two-milligram syringe, a squirt of naloxone in each nostril, ambu-bag and ventilation and then boom, they'd snap out of it. The stuff was like magic. I can't tell you how many people I've brought back from the dead. Whether they liked it or not."

"Mission Mountain," Billy said as he lit up one of the few remaining cigarettes from the pack. "Boarding school. When I first got my hands on it. I didn't know anything about it. And then it flipped me all around, saved me. Then I wanted to know everything there was to know about it." He flicked his ash into the mug, tapped the cigarette to it. "How long are you going to keep me here," Billy asked as he took another puff.

"You want to leave?"

"I don't know."

"We can get outta here, if you want. If you're feeling up for it. I, myself, am getting stir-crazy. And we should get started anyway. There's a big rally downtown today. They've been occupying Zuccotti Park. I need to see it. Need to begin. You should see it too. Get writing again."

Billy took a few last puffs from his cigarette and dropped the butt into the mug. "Ok." He went back into the bedroom, undressed and got into the shower. He turned the hot on all the way, wanted it to scorch his skin. As he stood there in the shower, he remembered his possessions: bubba, his pack, his supply.

He turned the water off, wrapped a towel around his waste, then searched around the room for his things. He looked under the bed and in the bedroom closet. Then he got more frantic. He searched through the kitchen, then through the living room of the railroad apartment. He opened cabinet doors, pulled things out, was ransacking the space. Bryan grabbed him from behind and held him tight.

"Relax, Billy, relax."

Billy pushed back and escaped out of Bryan's grasp.

"What did you do with my shit?"

"Okay, just hold up a second now, just wait a second…"

"No! What did you do with it! Where's Bubba!"

"Who?"

"Where the fuck is Bubba! Where the fuck is my bag!"

Bryan let go of him and walked over to the closet in the living room and slid the sliding door to it open. There sat his clothes, washed and folded, his sleeping bag rolled up on the bottom shelf, his bag on the floor, and Bubba leaning comfortably against the wall.

Billy looked down at his things in the closet, sitting there ever so peacefully, and he felt relief, then belly pains, then cold sweats. His body shook—it was coming. Bryan walked over to Billy and hugged him. Billy moaned into Bryan's shoulder.

"And what about the rest of it," Billy grumbled.

"That's all there was, Billy."

"No, what about my shit."

"There was no other shit, Billy."

"My fucking pills!" Billy felt his insides rising through his chest and thought he might vomit.

"There were no pills, Billy. Only empty bottles."

They continued holding each other. Bryan lifted Billy's head from his shoulder and turned Billy's face toward his.

With his two hands on Billy's cheeks, Bryan pulled Billy's face in and brought their lips together. Bryan pressed his lips hard against Billy's, and Billy's world continued to flash into darkness, his synapses darting in painful directions. Billy's towel fell to the floor. Bryan grabbed a hold of him and they did a sideward step movement into the bedroom, and they both collapsed upon the bed.

As Bryan was taking his shirt off, Billy flipped his naked body to the side and sat up. Vomit exploded out of his mouth and bubbled onto the floor at the side of the bed. Billy lay back down and rubbed his fingers over his temples.

"I need my pills. I'm sick."

Billy attempted to sit up again, but Bryan pulled him back to the bed and held him down as he wriggled from the pain underneath the pressure of Bryan's body.

Eventually, after Billy's worming around had ceased, Bryan let go of him and walked into the kitchen, got a mop and bucket.

Billy's eyes closed, and he may have passed out, but he wasn't sure for how long. When he opened his eyes, Bryan was standing over him, dressed in black.

"Today's, obviously, not the day for you to be joining

me. Soon, I'm sure."

Bryan exited the bedroom, locked the door behind him, and Billy was alone again.

The routine went on—time slipped by and days were morphing into each other. Billy slept during the day and sometimes at night, but it was never a full sleep. Bryan continued to leave the house every morning—Billy could hear the front door shutting—usually returning at night, but sometimes not coming back until the following evening. While awake, Billy felt warped, physically distorted. It felt as if his insides were being squeezed, twisted dry, like the tentacles of an octopus wrapping ever more tightly around his body. It was his father squeezing him, he felt, trying to communicate from the other side.

Sometimes, when Billy's moaning got loud, Bryan would unlock the door to the bedroom and hold him. Pet him. Calmed him as much as he could until the bout was over. Bryan did it like clockwork whenever he was home and heard it, out of habit, like Pavlov's dogs going to feed at the ringing of the bell.

On Friday morning, almost a week after Billy had been trafficked back to the city, Billy woke early—it was 5AM—his door was unlocked, and he went to the kitchen. Bryan was awake in the living room, already dressed in his black Occupy regalia.

"I'll make breakfast," Billy said.

He cooked up a simple but hearty meal for himself and for Bryan—scrambled cheesy eggs, toast with jelly, coffee, but it was the first time in a long time he had cooked anything. Billy ate everything on his plate. During breakfast, Bryan made reference to a girl at the protests who had gotten into the habit of flashing the police every time they came to break things up.

"She hasn't been arrested yet. Go figure."

Billy smiled candidly.

"You're ready," Bryan said. "Take a shower. It's time for you to get started."

Bryan turned on the shower for Billy, and he got in, then he got dressed in some of Bryan's clothes that he had put out for him. Billy drank another cup of coffee and smoked a cigarette while Bryan was in the other room with the door shut. Billy saw his cell phone on the kitchen counter, dead. He hadn't even bothered to plug it in. There was no one for him to talk to. When Bryan came out, he dropped a set of keys on the table and some rolls of twenty-dollar bills.

"Just in case we get separated. It can get pretty crazy down there. And today is going to be a big one. We're occupying all over the city. You and I are going to hit the Stock Exchange. Zuccotti Park got cleared out by the police. People are angry. We're going to go wreak some havoc."

Billy felt like a vampire when he walked out into the early morning daylight. The sun was blinding, and it took him a minute to get adjusted to it.

It felt good to be back on the train, to feel its vibrations. They got off at Wall Street with some time still before the rally was to begin. Pigeons were roaming the streets. Vendors were setting up their booths on the sides of the street and putting out their New York-related merchandise: "I Heart New York" t-shirts, Statue of Liberty and Wall Street Charging Bull statuettes, books, paintings, artwork of city sights and celebrities. He saw some tourists with cameras hanging around their necks. A Middle Eastern man was setting up his fruit stand and arranging the fruit from his truck onto the makeshift shelves. Businessmen and women were walking by briskly. Billy and Bryan walked over to the recently-vacated Zuccotti Park and stood on the sidewalk on the outskirts of it. Occupy Wall Street protesters, some dressed in black and some in pedestrian clothing, had started to surface.

And soon enough they were surrounded by the Occupiers, many with signs in hand. Bryan told Billy that in Louise Nevelson Plaza a few blocks away, the police were already lined up in their riot gear. Billy pictured the police standing there patiently in formation.

"Mike check!" one Occupier yelled to the crowd as loud as she could. People fell silent and turned their stares to the woman up front.

"Mike check!" the group of Occupiers in close proximity yelled back.

"Mike check!" other Occupiers in a section of people farther back from the first group yelled in unison.

"In a few minutes…" the first Occupier continued.

"In a few minutes…" the first group repeated.

"In a few minutes…" the group further back echoed for the rest to hear.

"We will walk as one unit…"

"We will walk as one unit…"

"We will walk as one unit…"

"As one unified tribe…"

"As one unified tribe…"

"As one unified tribe…"

"As the representation…"

"As the representation…"

"As the representation…"

"Of America's uninsured and underinsured…"

"Of America's uninsured and underinsured…"

"Of America's uninsured and underinsured…"

"Of America's unemployed and underemployed…"

"Of America's unemployed and underemployed…"

"Of America's unemployed and underemployed…"

Bryan and Billy, mixed in with the crowd, were in

close proximity to the Occupier who was shouting the commands for the others to repeat. Bryan was staring forward and chanting right along with her, and Billy, instead of looking forward, was staring to his right at his comrade. Bryan seemed suddenly taller and more muscular in that moment, with his hair falling over his ears and his busy beard dancing on his face to the tune of what he was yelling in unison with the others. Billy's hair was longer now and his beard thicker too, though still patchy in parts of his cheeks. He turned his attention to the protester as well but didn't chant along. Though he would from time to time whisper the chants, but it was clear that his interest was elsewhere, nowhere.

"Of America's indebted youth…" she continued.

"Of America's indebted youth…" shouted the second group containing Billy and Bryan, repeating the terms.

"Of America's indebted youth…" Billy heard rumble from behind him.

"Of America's disheartened and disenchanted…"

"Of America's disheartened and disenchanted…" Bryan screamed out with the others. He was yelling the chants now as loud as he could, rocking his fist in the air.

"Of America's disheartened and disenchanted…" came from behind him.

"We represent…"

"We represent…"

"We represent…"

"America's future!"

"America's future!"

"America's future!"

Another Occupier in black had appeared in front with the one leading the chants and now yelled with two fists in the air, "we are the ninety-nine percent!"

"We are the ninety-nine percent!"

"We are the ninety-nine percent!"

"We are the ninety-nine percent!" another voice yelled from the front.

"We are the ninety-nine percent!" group one repeated.

"We are the ninety-nine percent!"

"We are the ninety-nine percent!" the man up front shouted again. He could have yelled anything at this point, and they all would have repeated the words, with just as much vigor and enthusiasm.

The chants continued and eventually morphed into an indecipherable roar. Loud cheering and celebrating commenced. Many raised their hands into the air and wiggled their fingers upward quickly and energetically. Some raised their signs into the air and bobbed them up and down; some did it somewhat violently.

He heard the rumblings of it from people in the crowd: the police had begun their march from Louise Nevelson Plaza. In a sudden yet non-combative dash, the Occupiers flooded the streets and walked in loud unorganized groups toward the New York Stock Exchange.

In those few minutes before the ringing of the opening

bell, they occupied all of the street and sidewalk outside of the large Greek theatron-inspired building. Their presence was overwhelming. There were partitions set up in the street designated for the protesters, but once it was full, they aligned themselves all along other sections of the street and sidewalk and a group of them sat right in front of the New York Stock Exchange building blocking anyone from entering or exiting. Billy saw the police in riot gear circling around the group from all sides. The police force was one unified color while the Occupiers were made up of a wide array of colors peppered with black.

When 9:30AM hit and the opening bell rang inside the walls of the Stock Exchange, the Occupiers had a full-on human blockade on the sidewalk and into the street. They were cheering and yelling things, so many different things, just incomprehensible thundering in Billy's ears.

Then over the thundering a group of Occupiers shouted, "Banks got bailed out!"

"We got sold out!" others shouted out in response.

"Banks got bailed out!" the first group yelled again.

"We got sold out!" they were all now repeating.

"Banks got bailed out!" Bryan screamed, his voice cracking now from doing too much yelling, and Billy gazed up at a plane overhead.

The whole chamber was now belting out the refrain—Bryan too, with an aggression Billy had never seen before, and then Billy's eyes darted around at the police as they were breaking into the huddle.

"All day!"

"All night!"

"Occupy Wall Street!"

"All day!"

"All night!"

"Occupy Wall Street!" the orchestra continued on.

Officers were now a few feet in front of him, all around him. "You are in violation of blocking a public byway," he heard one of them bark to some of the sitting Occupiers. "Stand to your feet and move back!"

The sitting Occupiers didn't move from their positions, arms locked.

"If you don't stand up, we will be forced to physically move you from this area."

"We're not doing anything wrong! We're just sitting here!" a young woman yelled back.

"This is your last warning. Stand to your feet and move back!"

They did not comply.

One of the officers started the trend by lifting one Occupier up by the arm, cuffing him with plastic restraints and dragging him back to an area partitioned off by police vehicles. Other officers were now doing the same.

Bryan gave one of them a sideward stare. "Carabasa," Billy heard Bryan say to himself. Carabasa, Billy remembered, his ex-partner. Carabasa was grasping for one of the Occupiers' arms, but the Occupier dodged his advance and rolled to his side. Carabasa reached for his pepper spray, bent down and with a sideward squeeze, sprayed the Occupier in the face. The Occupier rolled onto his back and covered his eyes, screaming. Another officer slapped plastic restraints on his wrists and pulled him back to the partitioned area.

"You can't do that!" another yelled. "We are just exercising our rights. We have just as much of a right to be here as you do!" she yelled.

"Not here you don't, not today," an officer threatened back.

Billy watched as other officers pushed through the crowd to get closer to a chant circle in the middle of the street. One of the officers pushed a young guy with long hair out of his way. The guy paused for a moment, thought about what he was about to do, and then acted. He pushed back. Another one of them saw this and also started pushing. Before long, they were fighting back, throwing fists. Others saw the fighting and started fights of their own.

Billy heard one of the officers yell, "masks!"

"Masks!" other officers repeated.

"Masks!" even more echoed. Then tear gas was thrown into the crowd.

Many of the Occupiers ran for cover while others fought back harder than before. Blinding smoke took over; more grabbing and pulling, punching and kicking. Taserings and beatings with batons. Bryan ran forward into the smoke to get into the fight while Billy cowered in place. Bryan only got one good swing in before he got tasered, and he fell to the ground. He was breathless but stood back up as quickly as he could to not get trampled. His body was hunched over from the pain, and his eyes were closed. Billy's eyes were watery and red from the gas, and he wanted to get out of the smoke, but he also wanted to get to Bryan, wanted to help him, but there was so much violence between them, so he just stood there, frozen.

"That's a violation!" Billy heard Bryan screaming. "Violation 18653! Officer! Officer! 18653!"

"Larenterino! You stupid fuck!" someone yelled back at him.

Billy saw that it was Carabasa, and he got up in Bryan's face, then coldcocked him, hard, and Bryan fell to the ground. Other officers encircled around Bryan and swung at him with their batons. Billy watched in horror, yelled and screamed for them to stop.

"18653!" Bryan was moaning, covering his face with his body curled.

Billy bent down in place and wrapped his arms around his body, back inside himself, vacating his body and going somewhere else. When he returned, the smoke was settling and the chaos was over as if it had never even happened. Billy saw a line of police vans and officers loading them with some last Occupiers with their arms behind their backs.

Some Occupiers and non-Occupiers alike were standing at the barricades to the side of the vans, watching. Billy ran over to the barricades and watched as well. He scanned the crowd, tried peering through the vans' tinted windows but could only make out shadowy outlines of bodies. Behind one of the vans were some police cars. Three or four officers were huddled around one of the police cars, and in the backseat of it, with the window down, he saw him sitting there. Bryan's hands were behind his back and his bloody head was resting against the back of the seat, eyes closed. Billy watched as one of the officers bent over, tapped him through the window, was saying something to him, asking him something. Bryan opened his eyes and looked back at the officer but didn't say anything. He just stared back at the officer with an ominous glare. Blood dripped over his eye. His eyebrows were perched down. He rolled his head and surveyed past the officers over to the barricades. He saw Billy looking back at him. Their eyes locked. Bryan nodded at him confidently. "Write-it-down," he mouthed. "Write," he mouthed with a vigorous nod, "it," with another.

Soon the vans drove off, some of the police cars too, including the one that had Bryan. Onlookers were still hanging around, but the scene was over. Billy slowly walked back in the direction they had come that morning, past the street vendors and the merchandise booths, and he got back on the train. He looked at his hands, and they were shaking. His whole body was shaking.

He walked through the door of Bryan's apartment and sat down at the kitchen table. Just sat in silence. His journal was resting there in front of him, open to the first blank page toward the back of the book with a pen resting atop. No words were being written.

Then, sitting there, the tingles came whirring in. Once the tingles started, they wouldn't stop. The tingles turned into a throb; the throb turned into a pulsating alarm ringing and ringing in his ears and causing strophic red to come in and out of his vision. There was no denying it. He plugged in his phone and when it turned on, frantic fingers dialed an old pharma-connect.

22

He was chain smoking out of Bryan's window when he heard a pounding at the door. Billy got up, unlocked the clasp with fumbling fingers. When he opened the door, he saw his comrade standing there with dried blood crusted onto his face and on the sides of his mouth. His eyes were puffy and shiny with nodes of purple, red, and blue. His nose was swollen and looked broken. His clothes had dried blood painted onto them.

"Welcome home."

Bryan slowly walked into the apartment. He removed his blood-encrusted shirt and sneakers and fell upon the bed. The bedroom light highlighted his hairy face. He rolled over onto his belly and buried his face into the pillow. Billy sat on the corner of the bed, looked as though he were about to say something but remained silent, then just stared up at the white stucco ceiling.

Bryan flipped his body over quickly, after being dead

still. He sat up. "What a fucking massacre. And I knew some of them. Anders, and Perez too. Carabasa. Fucking Carabasa. They're probably at home fucking celebrating. They put Harry in a goddamn coma. And Mikey. Mikey probably has half a dozen broken ribs. They think they nailed me. They think they finally got me. They think they'll finally be able to put me away for good. They don't even know what's coming. I'm ashamed to have ever been associated with those monsters. Workhorses of our fascist system. Our freedom was in jeopardy, but now it's gone. Billy. Can't you see it? Of course you can. And so, it's time, Billy. I didn't think it would come so soon. It was not supposed to come this quickly. But it's here now. There was more to do. But it's my time now, Billy."

Billy's eyes shifted from Bryan's face back up to the white stucco. Through the haze that had taken him back over, Billy flashed back to what his comrade had spoken about in Appalachia.

"Billy, look at me. Look at me, Billy."

Billy slowly brought his eyes back to Bryan's.

"It's time, Billy. It's my time to make my mark. My time is now. This is it. Billy? Billy, do you understand?"

Billy continued to sit erect but now with lowered eyes. They sat silently on the bed. The realization was settling into Billy's mind. Tears were falling from Bryan's eyes, and he was smiling. Billy's dilated pupils were dry.

"Well then…"

Bryan opened his swollen eyes wide and brought a hand to Billy's face. He softly put his fingers under Billy's chin and raised his head up while turning it in his direction. Bryan brought his face close to Billy's and looked confidently into his eyes. If he realized that Billy had used again, it didn't phase him, for he had other, more important, personal issues pending.

"Tomorrow, Billy, I shall set myself on fire."

The words rolled out of his mouth easily as they continued to stare at each other.

Billy lost his composure when he saw the seriousness on Bryan's face and hyperventilated. Bryan embraced his comrade, wrapped his body around Billy's shaking body. Billy settled down finally after taking some deep breaths. He stood and faced out the window. He turned back around and stared up again at the white stucco ceiling.

"I guess I should cook us some dinner," Billy said, not knowing what else to say.

"No. I can't eat tonight. I'd like a hot shower though, I think. Maybe a little bit of whiskey."

Billy turned the shower on for Bryan. Billy looked at himself in the mirror studying the face before him, the image slowly shifting in shades of beige to red, elongating then shrinking in size. Bryan entered the bathroom quickly and grabbed onto Billy from behind. It startled him. Bryan laid kisses on Billy's neck and shoulder. Bryan rubbed his beard along Billy's back. Billy closed his eyes. Bryan undressed Billy and then took his own clothes off and walked him into the shower. Bryan washed him as the mirror steamed over. Bryan shaved Billy's face and body, and Billy remained motionless and calm and let the gentle feeling of being touched wash over him with the water.

The substances Billy had ingested earlier made him feel as though his synapses were firing properly again, but then, the urge to jerk the wheel came in heavy. And it sat there in his head, and it stayed.

His body humming, Billy said, "I'll do it with you."

Bryan stopped washing and let the water fall over his face with closed eyes. He then lifted his eyes and stared into Billy's.

"Billy. Oh, Billy. No, it's not your time. You have more to do, more to write. I need you…I need you to tell this story. The world needs you to tell this story. It's why we were brought together."

"My story is over."

Bryan shook his head with his eyes at their feet. "We'll go together, then," he said. "But I'll go first. And you'll stand guard to be sure no one gets in the way. Agreed?"

They both stood in the shower for a while longer. They sipped whiskey while drying off, put on robes and moved to the bed. They lay facing each other. They were silent. Bryan reaching for the bottle of whiskey. He took a big chug of it. Billy took a big chug of it too. He flinched, felt something inside, then slipped out of bed and went to the closet to his bag to the zippered pocket to his recently acquired narcotics. Popped, dropped, and returned. They turned to their sides and stared at one and other. Bryan got up to turn off the light. As he was reaching for the switch, he stopped himself. "Actually, no. I want to see you. For the last time."

Bryan removed his robe and crawled back into bed next to Billy. Bryan brought his eyes close to Billy's face and surveyed it, as if counting the number of pores. His head continued down Billy's body and his mouth kissed him from the nipples to the toes. The he turned off the lights and got back into bed.

There in the darkness, soon Billy felt weightless, levitating with Bryan in the middle of the room above the bed. Bryan brought his lips to Billy's and pushed hot air from his lungs into Billy's mouth, and they were interexchanging and carrying together the same makeup of nitrogen, oxygen, argon, and carbon dioxide, and their legs and their arms wrapped around each other, and it felt like Bryan's flesh was unwrapping from his body and cocooning the two of them together.

And they kept floating up. And there was no pain. He felt their bodies continue to rise as water continued to rise around them, and they rose through the sky, through space, into a throbbing darkness with bright neon wisps of smoke orbiting their floating metamorphosed self. The neon wisps drifting around through the darkness were colliding and fusing together and taking shape into a dark cephalopod figure with bright pulsating veins running down its body and tentacles, and he heard and felt the rapid thumping of his heart and with each thump the veins flared in color. Moaning, the shadowy octopoid figure reflected upon the dark blue water below with its muscular hydrostats snaking through it. Then it disappeared into the depths and it was just blackness again, still and silent. And in the blackness he felt his rapidly-beating heart now, and its drumming got louder as his and Bryan's body spun there in space and then fell like a droplet, plummeting back down to the watery wax below and into a vacuum-like alien membrane of watery moving parts with ticking gears, and sloshing through the anomalous device he felt their hairs untangle and their bodies pull apart, the polysepalous being ripping down the seams contorting him back into himself, still in darkness but weighted back down to the soft surface of the earth.

✕ ✕ ✕

Billy opened his eyes, and light from the early morning was shining through the windows. He blinked a few times. Bryan was next to him in bed and was also lying on his back. His eyes were wide open, and he was still, in a meditative state.

"How long have you been awake?"
"Not sure I slept."
Bryan intertwined his fingers with Billy's.

"I don't know if I'm dreaming," Billy said.

"Not a dream."

Bryan removed his naked body from the bed, and Billy closed his eyes again. He heard the sink faucet turn on in the bathroom. He heard the opening of a closet door from outside the bedroom. Then, just some stirring about in the other room. Bryan walked back into the bedroom, and Billy opened his eyes again. Bryan was in all black. He tucked his shirt into his pants, staring at himself in the mirror, and he brushed down his shirt so it was perfectly even all the way around.

"I laid your clothes out. I'll be right back." Bryan closed the apartment door behind him.

Billy got out of bed and picked up a few items off the floor. He walked into the kitchen, adjusted a few wall fixtures. He paced about in the apartment, then finally made his way over to the pile of clothes Bryan put out for him, and he slowly got dressed. While he was pulling his pants up, he was staring at the closet door.

He opened the closet, reached back into his pack and removed the pills that he had acquired the day before. He broke them up on the kitchen table and snorted them up his nose with one of the rolls of twenties Bryan had given him. He quickly wiped the remaining white dust off the table as he heard the front door opening.

Bryan walked in, and he had two jugs of gasoline in his hands.

"Told him my car ran out of gas."

Bryan removed two large plastic bags from the kitchen cupboard and put a jug in each bag. He wrapped them tight. He got out his backpack and Billy's backpack and placed the plastic bag-wrapped jugs into each bag. He stood, and Billy was also now standing, and they were silent for a moment, and Billy was shifting his weight from one foot to the other.

It felt to Billy like he was levitating again when they left the apartment, and flashes from the night before winked in. His body sailed after Bryan who was two steps ahead of him, down the street toward the train. They boarded the Manhattan-bound R at Roosevelt Avenue. The clock at the subway station read 7:47AM. They found open seats and sat down. Billy's eyes bounced from one person to the next.

"These are the people we're doing this for. And they have no clue what we're about to do for them. There's no mistake about it; we're at war. We're doing this for him," Bryan said while pointing with his eyes and a nod of the head at a man wearing a janitorial one piece under his jacket. "And for him." Bryan motioned toward a UPS worker. "And her." Bryan glanced at a woman reading out of a textbook. "And her." Bryan darted his eyes at a young lady playing on her cell phone. "See that boy by the door there. We're doing this for him."

Billy, in whisper, asked, "will it hurt?"

Bryan took out Billy's journal and pen from his pack and opened up to the first blank page. Billy's eyes widened when he saw his journal. Bryan wrote down the date at the top of the page and then in the middle of the page wrote:

I had finally started to see some semblance of progress toward a restoration of equality. But for every step in the right direction, I see five steps in the wrong. Things have fallen the wrong way. This is the time for a real course correction. In the right direction. I call the venerables, reverends of all religions and non, members of the Occupation and all the lay Americans to organize in full-solidarity to make sacrifices to protect what we hold sacred. We leave this world together, in unanimity. Without fear I go now to God. Long live the Occupation—Bryan Larenterino, Ex-Lieutenant of the 116th Precinct.

Bryan handed the journal and pen to Billy. Billy read Bryan's message, then sat still gazing off through the train windows for a few moments. Billy held the pen in his hand, but instead of writing, he just reread what Bryan had written. *Always have fallen the wrong way.* Billy handed the journal back to Bryan, and he slid it back into the backpack and zippered it closed. The train was more crowded now as it slowed down into the station.

"This is Fifty-Ninth Street," Billy heard over the train's loudspeaker.

Swaths of people entered the train. Bryan and Billy

stood to give a mother and her young child their seats.

"Stand clear of the closing doors please."

As the train continued to make its way downtown, Bryan and Billy got sandwiched in by the other passengers. Their bags were at their feet. They were both holding on to the pole and standing close to each other. Bryan's back was cramping up, and he winced for a second then stood back up straight. He saw Billy's face and smiled. They stood close to each other, almost as close as could be without kissing.

"This is Rector Street," he heard over the train loudspeaker.

The men in black with their backpacks on their shoulders walked through the turnstiles, past a police inspection table, and made their way up the flight of stairs to street level, eyes to the ground. They turned left onto Broadway and then their first right onto Wall Street. They were silent with each other.

When they got to the New York Stock Exchange, they surveyed the area of yesterday's carnage. A lot of the street was still partitioned off with metal dividers. Traces of blood had not yet been washed away from the streets.

They paused on the sidewalk and leaned against a metal divider. They took in the peaceful vision of the sun splashing its rays upon the neo-classical architecture. To their right, in front of Federal Hall, stood George Washington's bronze statue, reaching out its hand to the passers-by on the street.

"It may look unpleasant," Bryan said quietly, "but please do not panic. Death of any sort is a fearful thing to watch. You must not be scared by what you see."

Tourists were circling, many with cameras over their shoulders. Businessmen and women were making their way to their desks. Occupiers and non-Occupiers had surfaced, some with shabbier outfits and scruffier beards than others. Billy saw a few uniformed officers resting their backs against the wall of a building on the far end of the street, making small talk with each other. Vendors were stationed along the street. Some were already set up for operation, while others were in the process of assembling their tables. It was the same set of vendors, in addition to a few new ones, as yesterday. The fruit vendor was back, going through the same routine as yesterday, as if nothing had happened.

Bryan slid a lighter into Billy's front pocket. Bryan unzipped his backpack and opened the plastic bag containing the jug of gasoline. He removed the cap from the jug. Billy whimpered, feeling suddenly dead sober, caught himself and swallowed hard. The cap of gasoline left an oily residue on Bryan's fingers.

Bryan stared at the patch of cement which would become his final resting spot. To reassure himself of fire's potency, he lit his oily middle finger with the flame of his lighter; it lit up immediately, and he hardly reacted but for the twitching of his eyelid. He smothered his lit finger with his other hand. He looked at his finger, now a shade of black, with a calm appraisal. His eyes moved from his finger, down his hand to his wristwatch and the third hand was ticking closer to 9:30AM by the second. Bryan turned his gaze upon the giant red white and blue flag attached to the pillars of the New York Stock Exchange, and his eyes fixed upon it with an intense, eagle-eyed stare. His eyes flashed from one building to another, to city sights all around him, to the statue of George Washington. He turned his wide-eyed look to Billy and gave his comrade one final look, one final touch to his cheek.

The ringing of the opening bell sounded off inside the walls of the Stock Exchange. Bryan jumped the partition with no hesitation and walked ten quick paces toward the spot where he would sit, and as he walked he lifted his backpack above his head and turned it upside down. Gasoline poured over his head and body. He splashed it onto his clothes as he sat down cross-legged, dumped the rest into a puddle at his feet. He chucked the backpack to the side, and the journal tumbled out and landed at the feet of bystanders as they were now watching in fuddled wonderment at what this man was doing. Bryan reached into his pocket for the lighter, closed his eyes. Then sparked it.

His body went up into a flame instantly and completely without giving him a second to reconsider.

Billy immediately felt his body falling upwards, as

if gravity had been reversed, through ice and into the frozen lake close to his childhood home in Dundalk where his brother had taught him how to ice skate as a kid. Billy's breathing accelerated to an uneven tempo; his initial screech had stagnated to a dull hiss, even though he wanted to continue crying out, and he gasped for air as his body continued to fall and as Bryan's body continued to burn. Billy's heart beat violently inside his chest as the radiant colors before him danced large and the sheets of black smoke swirled into the sky. Billy had the sensation of his own ears and eyelids and lips and appendages ripping away, off his body, in a protracted persecution, as if it were his body on fire.

Billy continued to stare wide-eyed as his comrade was perishing before him, and it was already too late for rescue. He glanced around, suddenly *praying* for a familiar face, to lay eyes on that familiar face, but instead only saw the faces of the strangers in the crowd, also standing by in awe around the fire in the street, like 350 monks encircling Thích Quảng Đức himself. The partitions were getting knocked over and trampled upon as people pushed and shoved to try to get a better look at the incineration. Many didn't even seem to know it was a human body that was aflame; instead it looked like some other inanimate object that needed extinguishing. Only a minute and a half had passed when Billy heard the ringing of distant fire trucks. It got louder as it got closer, and he felt the alarm bells in his bones with every breath he breathed and every throb of his pulse. His synapses were darting in every which direction, malfunctioning and coo-cooing like that of an old grandfather clock spun up to light speed.

Billy watched as Bryan's vacant body fell forward into a pile, and he was gone now, Billy could see, out of this world and on to the next. What once was was now gone, and the ringing of the fire trucks muffled out, the world went mute, and the palpitations eased. And he looked down and watched as his fingers were untwisting the cap to the jug of gasoline inside his bag. And he watched how his hands were now pulling the jug of gasoline out of the bag, and how they raised the jug in the air. How his hands turned the jug upside down, and then the cool liquid was washing over his head and his face, watching how it splashed over his arms and body and legs and feet.

Billy fell forward to his knees, and his eyes stung from the gasoline and the smoke of his comrade's burning remains, and he inhaled the smoke. He watched the wet cement move below him and past him as his body crawled closer to the heat, and when an arms-reach away from what was left of Bryan, Billy curled his body into a ball.

Now to finally taste the true bitterness and sweetness of that for which he had been striving to experience his whole young adult life—what had been tasted only faintly through ingestion, inhalation, snorting, and injection—now to savor fully, to ignite every single pore on his person. Looking up through burning blurred eyes, through the smoke, and then far beyond the confines of the earth's ozone, he saw the long-faced father reaching down with his long tentacles for an embrace, softly whispering that it was now time for Billy to solve the riddle.

23

He felt an arm wrap around his chest and yank his body backward, and his legs dragged upon the pavement. He felt his body being lifted off the ground, heard the familiar voice say, "hang tight, Little Shrimp." The sound of the commotion all around him, the indistinguishable voices and the screams, it all came flooding back in sharply through his ears after having been shut out by the transcendent glow of stifling damp smoke. His body was spun around, ripped away from the burning corpse he was ready to clasp for an embrace. His shoulders and arms brushed up against other bodies in the crowd, and hands were grabbing at him, but he felt himself pull free with quick jerks and twists until the grabbing stopped. Jagged movements were making his arms flail beneath his body; his head bounced limply in sync with running footsteps. With his vision blurry and wet from the smoke, all he could see as his body spun around were fuzzy shades of hordes of bodies, now growing smaller in the distance. He felt the warmth of the broad heaving chest of the one carrying him.

He watched as slabs of sidewalk cement below him were quickly shifting into each other underneath his body as he floated past them. He was coasting down different streets, swinging around street corners, and he could suddenly make out Chinese on street signs, and the pungent smell of raw fish was at his nostrils with each breath, and before each exhale came the aftertaste of the gasoline which was still wet on his clothes and body. He was now moving down an alleyway, Chinese on the walls of the buildings to his left and right, then at the end of the narrowed alleyway his body dropped to the ground and all was still. He heard the voice say, "be strong, Little Shrimp," and he shut his eyes.

Then he opened them. And he was alone.

He sat up. And he saw the whole scene play out again in his head. He watched as Bryan's body went up into flames. He watched him scream, watched his head still twitching through the black smoke, and he watched Bryan's body collapse forward. He watched as he got closer and closer and hotter and hotter until he could just reach out and grab him.

And then he remembered being yanked back. And he remembered being pulled away from the flames. *Peter.* And he saw it was Peter's arms yanking him back, Peter hoisting him up and holding him to his burly body, Peter carrying him to safety, his eyes staring down at him. But now he was alone, in some grimy Chinatown alley behind a dumpster.

He remembered again the people in the crowd grabbing at him, and he suddenly saw himself pulling his arms free from them, his own hands pushing them out of his way. *It was you, you that was fighting past them.* He suddenly saw his feet, his own feet, sprinting forward on the concrete, one foot after the other. *And you were the one running.* For Peter had not ripped him back from the flames; it was Billy who had yanked his own body back. It was Billy that had fought through the crowd. It was Billy running down those streets, hustling around those street corners. It was Billy, and Billy alone, who had taken refuge here in this alleyway. He had saved himself.

✕ ✕ ✕

He sat in that alleyway until nightfall, hiding behind the dumpster, afraid to come back out into the light of day. But he finally emerged, and still in all black, blended into the darkness of night.

A last roll of twenties was still in his pocket. He found a subway station, bought a MetroCard, took the train to Queens, kept his head down. On Bryan's block he saw the police officers standing outside of his apartment building. Billy stopped there on the corner and watched from behind a tree. Soon a few more officers came out of the building. Others went in. He got a little closer. It was Carabasa who had come out.

Do they want you too? No, you didn't do anything. Or, did you? No, you didn't kill anybody. He did it to himself. How would they even know you were involved in any of this? Then he remembered his cellphone, sitting on the counter, and he thought that they must have already dissected it, through and through. He pictured them dusting the whole place for prints, dusting down Bubba. Then he thought of the surveillance cameras scattered across the city—how they've probably scoured through footage already of their morning journey, put out an APB for the martyr's accomplice, that right here and now cameras could be locked in on him. He ducked his head, turned and quickly walked away. He remembered the journal, remembered Bryan writing his final remarks down on the train, remembered the journal flying out of Bryan's bag after he chucked it to the side before setting himself on fire and it landing at someone's feet. *They must have it. Someone must have gotten it. Bryan's suicide note. And every fucking thing that you wrote.* He suddenly felt naked, exposed, all his secrets revealed to the world.

He saw the entrance for the Roosevelt Avenue train station, and unsure of where else to go, walked down the steps and through the turnstile while keeping his head down low. When the E train came into the station, he boarded it, sat at the window, dropped his chest to his knees, his head in his hands. Then he reached into his pocket and took out the money roll and counted what he had left in his lap. Four twenty dollar bills, nine singles. Just enough to escape.

Billy saw he was riding the train in the wrong direction, toward its last stop in Jamaica, Queens. He knew he needed to get back into Manhattan in order to get past the city limits. He got off at Van Wick and reentered on the other side to catch a Manhattan-bound train. He saw on the map behind his seat that his train would make a stop at Port Authority Bus Station in midtown. He tapped the spot on the map with his finger, then sat back down and curled inward again. He would dart his eyes around through his fingers over his face at the people on the train to see if they were looking at him. To see if they recognized him. But no one was looking. No one cared.

He got off the train at 42nd Street, and standing across from Port Authority, he saw some officers on guard outside the building. He was too scared to walk past them, so he kept walking, through the bright lights of Times Square.

He walked past a discount clothing store with racks of clothes on the sidewalk. He stopped, turned back around and quickly flipped through the clothes on the hangers. He found a blue hooded sweatshirt for eight dollars and brought it inside to pay, and loud Afro-Caribbean music was playing from speakers on the wall. Behind the counter were hats for sale. He asked for the black New York Yankees one. He didn't make eye contact with the woman behind the counter. He wondered if she could smell the gasoline on his clothes.

Billy squeezed the rim of the hat to make it tight around his head while walking back to the bus terminal. He kept the hat low over his eyes, but not too low to raise any suspicions. He walked through the doors and kept his head down. He kept walking with his body tensed, thinking that he would be tackled to the ground at any second. But he kept walking and nothing happened. He finally turned around behind a column by the Au Bon Pain concession stand, and he looked back at the entrance. But no one was watching him. No one cared.

He found a bathroom. A few homeless men were washing up at the sink, and many of the stalls were occupied. He felt momentarily comforted by the stink. He took off his hat and sweatshirt and then the black long-sleeve shirt, washed all over with soap, gargled soap water. He threw the black shirt into the trash bin and put the sweatshirt and hat back on.

To the far corner of the Greyhound ticket counter were the self-service ticket kiosks. He scrolled through to see what buses were leaving that night. The options were numerous, and he had just enough money for a one-way ticket out of there.

His ticket printed along with the receipt, and he was left with seven dollars and some change. With a few hours before his bus's scheduled departure, he walked out of the terminal, past the guards again with his head down to his feet, and used what was left of his money for a combo meal at the Burger King across the street—got a Whopper with fries and a Coke. Food had never tasted so good.

After walking back into the station, this time with his head held a little higher, he sat in a corner against the wall at the departure gate, waiting to board his bus. His head pulsed heavy, and he was still seeing fire. He thought about the last time he had been waiting for a bus, when he met Bryan, and he just couldn't get his face out of his head, what it looked like then and what it looked like this morning as it was melting off his skull. And he thought of Peter—Peter pulling him back from the fire, but no real Peter at all. He was waiting for someone else to approach, kept looking around for wandering eyes in his direction, for someone to take interest in him and ask him about his life, about his writing. But no one came. No one cared.

He got up and strolled, and the loose change jingled in his pocket. Then he went on a hunt for a payphone. He walked up a flight of stairs, saw a series of them. At the payphone at the end of the row, he lifted the receiver and put it to his ear. He reached into his pocket and pulled out all the change that was left. Seventy-six cents. He inserted the two quarters, the two dimes, and the nickel into the coin slot and left the remaining penny on top of the phone box. He dialed the number. The operator's voice recording came on and informed him he had six minutes for the call before having to pay an additional twenty-five cents for another two minutes. Then it was ringing. Then he heard his voice say hello.

"Peter, it's me."

"Little Shrimp."

Then neither of them spoke.

"I was starting to think you might be dead," Peter said, breaking the silence.

"Still here."

"I must have left you half a dozen voicemails. What's this number you're calling me from?"

"Doesn't matter. I don't have much time."

"You're in New York?"

"For now. Not for long."

"What do you mean? Where are you going?"

"Doesn't matter."

Then more silence.

"I might be in some trouble."

"What kind of trouble?" Peter asked.

"I don't know. Things went kind of sideways after I saw you."

"I know about the accident. In the mountains. Your friend Bryan called me. He told me. He said he was helping you. That you were helping him with something, too, something important."

"He's gone, now."

"Gone?"

"Gone."

"Gone where?"

"Just…gone. I was almost gone too. But you…you pulled me back."

"Pulled you back? Pulled you back from what? You mean got you help? You talking about '08? The clinic?"

"I'm not talking about Baltimore. It was just this morning. I can't explain it, but you saved me, Peter. You really saved me this morning."

"I was at work this morning, dude. I don't know what you're talking about. You're not making sense, Shrimp. Unless…you had another accident this morning? Is that what's going on? What kind of trouble are you in?"

"I'm ok, Peter. Now I'm ok."

"Damn it, Shrimp—this is exactly why I didn't want you looking for him. Why I didn't want you to see him. For you to have another accident."

"I know, Peter."

"I mean, why the fuck did you want to find him anyway? You were doing good, finally doing good."

Billy thought about how to respond, wasn't quite sure of the answer. But he tried: "When Dad came back from Iraq, he was fucking ruined. And he kept falling further. You think I would've been happy. That the old man was finally getting what was coming to him. But when Cynthia called me and told me he had run off, I guess in the back of my head I knew where he was going all along, what he was planning, and I had unfinished business with him I guess, needed to finish it with him before it was too late. Just to say goodbye and go fuck yourself one last time—for the first time. But it's ok now. I'm ok with him being gone. I saw him, in my own way, yea I saw him, got some of that closure, I guess. I was doing some writing, actually—and that's kinda where I found him, where I got my closure. But now that he's dead, I guess it doesn't really matter."

"Billy. He's not dead."

Billy's eye shot up from the ground. "He's dead. That's what you told Bryan."

"I never told him he's dead."

"Yes, you did."

"No. I didn't."

"He said that you asked him how I found out about it."

"Yea, how you found out he was doping again."

"Doping? What are you talking about?"

"What I'm talking about is that you guys are all fucking junkheads, you know that? All three of you—you, him and Cynthia."

"He's not dead?"

"No. He's not dead. He's in some inpatient clinic in New Orleans. Maybe he was thinking about offing himself. Maybe he even tried. I don't know. But he's a resilient motherfucker. A lucky motherfucker. Both, probably. Just like you. Both of you—walking right up to that edge, basically touching it."

Billy didn't respond. Couldn't respond. Couldn't get words out.

"He told me he was trying to get clean when he came here. But I think he was using the whole damn time he was on the move. Or maybe he just started up again after he saw me. I don't know. Doesn't really matter now. And you too—you told me you were staying clean. That you were clean as a whistle."

"I've never been clean," Billy said softly after a pause, his eyes closed.

"You were clean once. I know you were. I also know he was the one that did it to you—that brought you into the fire in the first place. Shrimp—listen to me. You're better off apart. We all are. Some families are just not meant to be together."

Billy's eyes still closed, the glow-in-the-dark ceiling stars were there for him suddenly, in his bed back in Dundalk. Alan crawling in. And Peter sitting up in his bed across the room and watching.

"Why didn't you do anything?" Billy said, after another long pause.

"What are you talking about?"

"You just sat there. You always just fucking sat there."

Peter didn't say anything.

"You were always his guy, his little partner in the

back. You just fucking watched."

"Shrimp. No. I'm not doing this again."

"How could you have just sat there and watched."

"I'm going to hang up."

"Yea—just like always. Go ahead. Just go ahead. Retreat."

"Goddamn it, Shrimp!" Peter screamed. Then he was silent again. Then in a very measured low tone—"I was a fucking kid. Just a fucking kid. What was I supposed to do? I didn't fucking know what to do. I thought this shit was normal. That this was what families did."

They were silent again.

"It wasn't just you, Shrimp. It was me too."

More seconds passed. Then the operator's voice recording chimed in: "Please deposit twenty-five cents for the next two minutes. If twenty-five cents is not deposited in the next twenty seconds, your call will be automatically terminated. Thank you."

They both stayed quiet.

"Peter?"

"What is it."

And the phone went dead.

× × ×

It was just before 1AM, and the bus had pulled in. He waited at the door. It was just him and few stragglers pacing about behind him. He found a seat on the back of the bus and when it geared up to leave, it was nearly empty. The bus pulled out of the terminal, and he got one last glimpse of the city before the bus entered the Lincoln Tunnel.

After the bus came out on the other side, the city now behind him, his body was already easing to the bus's vibrational motion. He was escaping, but this one felt different because he had reached the very bottom of the well. He was the empty set, at last the true cardinality of zero, holding nothing, not one bottle nor bag of any kind of psychoactive substance on his person, not one dollar to reap any more of it, not one possession but the underwear and socks on his body, the pants and shoes with the lingering smell of petrocarbon, the sweatshirt and the hat holding in his head. Secrets dispelled, words set free.

The drugs inside his body worn thin and vacating, a sudden foreboding set in, and he thought of his hollow body stiffening to sheer neutronium, becoming that mythic chemical element zero, the collapsed core of a neutron star that was once the brightest sun in the cosmos, with neutrons upon neutrons clumping together by ever-more intense gravity till being crushed completely and his nucleus fully devoid of charge. *But the empty set is still a set*—and he smiled ever so briefly, neutrons spreading out and populating the universe, gravity releasing, breathing steady. For the charge was present and he was feeling it and he was it, and it was living; it was the cushion of his seat, the linoleum at his feet, the vibrations of the tires moving on cement lulling his insides with a heart beating firm and pumping an even flow of blood through his arteries to his organs to the whole of his body, now being transported forward in time, seventy miles per hour, further and further, or closer and closer, but he couldn't say which.

ACKNOWLEDGMENTS

To Dad and Mom, who are not one thread like the parents portrayed in this book—this work would not have been possible without your unwavering love and support. You haven't let a single day pass without loving me unconditionally. I want you both to know that you are the most wonderful people I have ever met, and I feel so very proud to be your son. *Thank you. I love you.* Mike and Julia—you both inspire me every day. To be born into this family has been my life's greatest blessing. Charlotte—I was so unbelievably lucky to have found you, back when this book was just a distant dream. You've made me a better person. A more empathic person. You've shown me how to be a better observer of the world and a more active participant within it. Linsey, writer-editor-teacher extraordinaire—you have been a true mentor; I could always depend on you to help right this ship when it was taking on water. I wouldn't be the writer and teacher I am today without you. Thank you to the Vermont Studio Center and the City College of New York, where much of this writing took place, to the collective of writers at Global City who were an invaluable resource in helping me shape the work in its final stages, to Karen, for steadfastly championing my work, to the whole Rochon crew, and to the Tantas and the whole mishpucha. And to Wesley and little Louisa—don't ever forget: *i carry your heart(i carry it in my heart)*.

David Puretz is the Editorial Director of the literary magazine Global City Review and the creator and founder of burly bird zine. He teaches writing at Yeshiva University in New York City, where he currently resides. The Escapist is his debut novel.

CPSIA information can be obtained
at www.ICGtesting.com
Printed in the USA
LVHW012112170120
644012LV00004B/482